The Sheriff's Christmas Angels

THE SHERIFF'S CHRISTMAS ANGELS

DEBRA HOLT

The Sheriff's Christmas Angels
Copyright © 2017 Debra Holt
Tule Publishing First Printing, December 2017

The Tule Publishing Group, LLC

ALL RIGHTS RESERVED

No part of this book may be used or reproduced in any manner whatsoever without written permission except in the case of brief quotations embodied in critical articles and reviews.

This is a work of fiction. Names, characters, places, and incidents are products of the author's imagination or are used fictitiously. Any resemblance to actual events, locales, organizations, or persons, living or dead, is entirely coincidental.

ISBN: 978-1-948342-03-2

Dedication

The Sheriff's Christmas Angels is my first holiday romance. I wanted to revisit McKenna Springs for this heartwarming story. All the ingredients are here… two hearts searching for their counterpart, an adorable child wishing for a mother, a lost puppy in need of her forever family, and all believing in the power of love and wishes made to a Christmas angel.

I am dedicating this book to my family who taught me about the joys and the miracles of the Christmas season based in love and unending faith and hope. And especially to my grandmother, Sallie Mae Hannum, who taught me about the magic of wishes made to Christmas angels. I believed with a simple child-like faith then and to this day, there is an angel placed first on our Christmas tree before any other decorations. And quite a few wishes go along with her placement.

The story I wrote also highlights another belief that was instilled in me by my grandmother. That is the belief that people come into our lives often when we never expect them, but when we need them the most. We might not realize their purpose at the time, but they are often answers to our prayers and needs. Such is the case for the Drayton family in this book and for Emma, and even little Angel. All their lives intersecting by chance, but bringing such love and joy where most needed.

My Christmas wish for each of you this season is that you may find the peace and joy of the holiday and hold it in your heart all year long. And may you know the true treasure of Christmas angels in your own life.

Happy Holidays,
Debra

Prologue

"CHARLIE NEEDS A mother and you need a wife. It's high time you realized that."

Cole Drayton slammed the milk carton back on the shelf and shut the refrigerator door none too gently. He let out an exasperated grunt in reply while trying to temper the words that wanted to fly from his mouth. They were words that would probably get his mother headed after him with a bar of lye soap in her hand.

He took a couple sips of the coffee to let his thoughts simmer down. He wished he had just kept going past the turnoff to the house and gone on to the diner in town instead of coming into his kitchen a few minutes ago for another cup of coffee. That was when he had found his mother already seated at his breakfast nook... lying in wait for him. A deep breath drawn inward gave him patience to maintain an even tone with her.

"I *had* a wife. It didn't work out all that well, if you recall. We keep having this conversation and the outcome is always the same. I realize you mean well, Mother. But this is *my* life... mine and my daughter's and—"

"And you want to keep your head buried in the sand. Look around you, Cole. You work from sunup to sundown. You weren't busy enough helping your dad run the cattle operation while he farmed our place, you had to step in and fill Riley's shoes as acting sheriff of this county when he got hurt in that car wreck a few months back. Your child is either with a daycare worker or me. And I'm getting older by the day and can't do all the things with a child that a younger woman can. Not to mention this house needs a thorough cleaning more than once in a blue moon. It might as well be a hotel with all the lack of personal touches and the—"

"Running a ranch and being a sheriff, interim or not, doesn't leave a lot of time for interior decorating. This house suits us just fine the way it is. Are you telling me that you don't want to keep Charlie any longer? I'll find someone to come in and take care of her if you need a break."

"And where will you find a reliable person to do that between here and Frost Creek? It's easy to say the words, but the reality of doing it is another story and next to impossible. There're mighty slim pickins' between the farmers and ranchers' wives and the old maids. Most able-bodied, younger women are career-minded and drive into Austin or San Antonio to work or have gone off to college."

"Exactly true with finding a wife… even if I ever wanted one of those again. Which I do *not*. Or do you have one of those old maids you mentioned in mind for the job?"

"It would be a heck of a job, too… putting up with the

likes of your hardheadedness. She'd need the patience of Job and the hide of an Arkansas mule." Mae Drayton's voice softened as she gazed at the tall man leaning against the cabinet across from her. "Son, you're working yourself too hard trying to escape something that isn't there any longer. Pamela's leaving you like she did shouldn't color how you see all other women. Charlie needs a woman's touch here and especially as she grows older. I'm not saying put an ad in the newspaper, but just open your mind to thinking about it and become more amenable. In the meantime, I'll keep my eyes open for someone, too, who could come in here and help with Charlie and the house. And if I find someone, promise me that you'll keep an open mind and give it a good try. Promise?"

That brought a pair of gray eyes straight to hers along with the scowl lines in his forehead. "No, Mother. You keep your eyes to yourself and do not go looking for more trouble for me. It's time you left to pick up Charlie, and time I got back to work."

He set the coffee cup into the sink and straightened, grabbing his hat off the back of the chair. Sliding it on his head, he moved to the backdoor, and then paused.

He gave her one more level look. "If you want to really help me out, find a good computer-literate person to get that mound of paperwork off my desk. The cattle accounts are behind going in the books by a couple of months or more since I don't have the time or patience to deal with it all when I do get home. That's something you can do *with* my blessing. As for the other… *I mean it, Mother.* Leave my personal life alone. I'm doing just fine on my own." The closing of the door behind him put a period at the end of the discussion.

She rose and moved to the window to watch her son's retreating back as he crossed to his white SUV with the markings of Chisos County Sheriff on its side. *Just like his father.* Cole was in a "mood" and needed some space. She knew him well enough to know he would head down the flat highway, let the window down, and turn up the radio that only ever played old rock 'n roll songs from the fifties. That had been his grandfather's doing in teaching him to listen to the oldies stations from the time he could walk good enough to go off with him in the older man's red and black truck… the same one he had restored and sat in the garage now. Her son needed some shaking up from the normal routine… heck, he needed just some shaking period!

Her mind was already working on a plan. She wasn't certain what the plan would look like, but she had to do something. Her heart ached for Cole and little Charlie. The house was too quiet and too empty… even when they were both in it. Her son was moving through life but not living it. She had to do something and time was not going to slow down. She had to believe that somehow, someway an answer to her prayers would be sent. She just had to keep believing there was a miracle out there somewhere.

Chapter One

In the space of less than an hour, the sunshine had disappeared as the dark midnight blue of the first "blue norther" barreled down from Canada across the mid-section of the country. Temperatures dropped almost thirty degrees in less than an hour over this portion of the edge of the hill country of Texas. The wind had whipped around and increased to a blustery forty miles per hour, with gusts adding another ten or so miles on to that number. Brown tumbleweeds raced and bounced over the fields and across the roadway ahead of her.

The wind threatened to push the battered green pickup off the blacktop. Emma Cramer increased her grip on the steering wheel, her hands already cramped. Now and then she released long enough to wipe a sweaty palm along her jeans' leg. The heater worked sporadically but was useless for the most part. With very little funds left in her pocket, there would not be any repairs to be had anytime soon. She would just have to add an extra layer of clothing or two, at her next fuel stop. *Being resourceful.* That was what her mother had called it.

Growing up, if there were awards to be given out for the "most resourceful"… her family would win it hands down. At least that was how it felt to be in a household of too many debts and never enough money. If there was anything to be counted on, it was the fact that tomorrow could, and often would, be worse than the day before. She had grown up waiting for the other shoe to drop, which it invariably always had. Her eyes gravitated to the falling fuel gauge. She had to stop soon.

Reaching over, she turned the radio up a bit. There was too much darkness around her, in the graying skies and the thoughts in her head. She had hit on the oldies-but-goodies station a little while back and that had been a bright spot. While her mother had waited on tables, it was usually these oldies that the juke box played in the country truck stops, and Emma had found herself taking a liking to the upbeat music. That was one holdover from her childhood that hadn't been a dismal memory. At the moment, they were playing a tune by the Beach Boys… something about a little deuce coupe. She tried to hum along with it to bring her mind to another place, but it didn't last long. Not even the music could get her mood to lighten.

What doesn't kill you makes you stronger. She had been brought up with that southern platitude ingrained in her DNA. If that was the case, she was the strongest person to escape from Harlan County. At age eighteen, she had been handed her high school diploma, stepped off the stage, and then went to the cemetery the next day to bury her mother.

Grace Cramer had survived two husbands, one an alcoholic and the other a paroled abuser, had buried one child and raised another. She had worked every odd job she could find to keep a roof over their heads after she had left her second husband in the dead of night when Emma was nine. But all those years of hard life caught up with her when Emma had begun high school. By the time her senior year came along, her mother didn't have any more strength left in her when colon cancer hit and moved quickly to take her.

At age eighteen, standing beside the cheap coffin that held her mother's remains, she had vowed that somehow the future was going to be different... no matter what she had to do or how long it took. She would find the better life her mother always told her was just around the corner. All Emma had to do was *believe*. Well, ten years later, she had little else but her belief, and it was getting harder each day to hold on to it.

As the sky darkened ahead, so did Emma's thoughts as they returned to memories of her life years ago. The trailer she and her mother lived in wasn't theirs. The furniture was patched and wouldn't even pay a junkman the gas it would take to pick it up for disposal. Emma had packed a few personal items into two cardboard boxes and gave the rest to neighbors in the trailer park or to the local Goodwill store. She put the silver chain with the small cross on it around her neck. That had been her mother's only jewelry... an heirloom from her own grandmother and mother.

It and the old, worn photograph of the guardian angel, hovering over two small children while a storm raged outside her wide-spread wings, were the items her mother had made certain to hold on to during each move. Emma had often studied the angel in the photo as a child. She wondered if there were real angels and how did she find one? Silly musings of a child. The photo and necklace were the two items she carried with her now. The sum total of Emma's life and her family fit in the back seat of the old truck. Then she had left the cemetery and Frost Creek in her rearview mirror. That was then… and this was now.

Here she was, on her way back… a sort of pilgrimage to her past as she moved toward a future she had fought hard to achieve. Besides the cross, the bible, and the newer, yet still used pickup she had purchased a couple years before, she had a piece of paper that proved she had graduated from the community college in Corpus Christi, with a degree in office management and computer systems. It had taken her longer than most students since she had to hold down two jobs, one in a church nursery school three days a week and one at the discount store's graveyard shift, four evenings. Between making money for school and going to classes, there had been no time for anything else. And before she had saved enough money to get in the door of the school to begin with, she had worked three years as a beautician and a waitress.

After graduation, she had been placed in a job in the

business office at the local hospital. It was a job and it paid. But there was still an empty restlessness inside her and so she had saved what she could to make the trip to Dallas to interview for two jobs that would finally pay enough for her to realize the benefit of having that degree. Her phone interviews for each had been successful and earned her the callbacks that set her out on the road toward the future she dreamed of having for so long. Maybe she was on the road to finding where she belonged and could actually put down solid roots for the first time in her life. It was both lonely and scary... to have come from nowhere and not be sure of where she was headed. That was okay with her. She knew what she had left behind so whatever lay ahead had to be better.

The flash of a red light from the dashboard brought her attention in a heartbeat. *Are you serious?* Her heart plummeted in her chest. "This can't happen... not now."

Simultaneously, her brain hopped from what she had left in her bank account to where she was in relation to her destination. Not for the first time, she derided herself for making the out-of-her-way detour to her old hometown. She should have stuck with the safest, straight shot major highway, instead of being on a two-lane back country road. She doubted she would even reach Frost Creek, much less Dallas. Her eyes began searching the distance ahead for some sign of a service station or hint of civilization.

Rolling plains and hills stretched to the horizon in all

directions, here and there the alternating rows of idle farmland broke the scenery along with patches of treed land and taller grassland pastures. Emma fought down the growing sense of unease at her situation. *Keep calm and think it through.*

"Please let me find a gas station and not be stranded on the side of the road," she begged aloud in the silence of truck.

She had gotten used to having her own voice as her companion in most cases. It was moments such as this that she felt the sudden wish for someone tangible to reach out to for help… for some degree of comfort knowing one wasn't totally alone. But there wasn't anyone but herself in that truck. Not even the Elvis tune playing on the radio could turn things around. His soulful voice just made it worse. She punched the button and silence was a deafening roar.

At that moment, her gaze lit on a tall sign and as she neared, she saw it was attached to the roof of a small, older building that was a convenience store with two fuel pumps standing out front. She doubted there would be a garage or mechanic to be found there, but at least it was a starting point.

Emma pulled the truck in front of the first pump and shut off the engine, silently praying she would be able to start it again once she fueled up. She stepped out of the truck, immediately grabbing the front of her denim jacket and hastily buttoning it against the strong wind with its chilly bite. Making a mental note to retrieve her wool cap from the bag in the back of the truck to keep her ears warmer, she hurried past the only other vehicle visible, a newer model SUV, parked next to the building.

A bell jangled over the door as she stepped through it. A gray-headed man, probably in his seventies, sat on a stool behind the counter to her right with a newspaper spread open on the counter in front of him. He looked up with a smile on his weathered face and nodded.

"Mighty windy out there... mind you don't blow away. You'll end up in New Mexico if you do."

She gave a return smile. "I'll keep that in mind." Moving closer to the counter, she withdrew her wallet from her pocket, sliding a twenty over the counter. "I need some gas. And I need to know where I might find the closest garage or mechanic? I've got a warning light that came on about five miles back and need to get it checked."

"Hmmm... there's a mechanic about twenty miles on down the road. Abel Bassey. He has a shop in McKenna Springs. But not sure he'll be around when you get there. He's also an emergency lineman for the power company and there're some lines down in the eastern part of the county. I heard he'd been called out earlier today."

"Guess I'll have to take my chances. Thanks for the information. By the way, do you have a ladies' room available?"

"Sure do. It's around the corner of the building outside—added them on last spring. You might have to wait a minute or two, there's another customer ahead of you."

"Thanks, again."

"You have a safe trip down the road, little lady."

Emma still had the smile on her face as she left the building and opted to pump her gas first. Making her way around the back of the building a few minutes later, she didn't see anyone else and, after a brief knock on the door with no reply, figured the other patron had gone around the other way. At least Emma wouldn't have to waste time standing and waiting in the cold.

Upon her exit from the restroom, she took a couple of steps when a pleading voice carried across to her on the wind, stopping her and holding her attention. An older woman stood at the entrance to what looked like an old, dilapidated garage, situated at the edge of the back-fence line about twenty yards to her right. Half her body was wedged inside the small opening that didn't look all that safe, the door hanging lopsided on one side. From the tone of her voice, Emma could tell she was worried. Emma hesitated for a second, she could ignore the little voice in her head and get moving on down the road… or not. *Pushover.*

She crossed the gravel area toward the woman. If anything, the temperature was dropping and the lady really didn't need to be out in it with her light sweater around thin shoulders. Emma judged her age to be mid-sixties to early to seventies maybe, with simply-styled white hair in a short length. Something about her brought a remnant of a memory of her mother.

"Excuse me," Emma said, announcing her presence. "Is there a problem I can help with?"

Instant relief showed in the light gray eyes turned in her direction. "Oh, my. Could you? I can't get through this space... and my granddaughter went in there after some stray puppy and I'm having a time trying to get her out."

Emma looked at the cracked wood of the door. "I don't think we can trust trying to open it any farther—it might fall off the track totally if we did that. What's her name?"

"Charlie... Charlene, actually. But we all call her Charlie. She's five going on fifteen sometimes... and stubborn as her dad, too."

"Well, let me see if I can crawl through the space."

"Please be careful," the woman said, as Emma went down on her knees, and looked at the opening. "Here, take my gloves so the gravel won't cut your hands." The woman quickly shed the caramel leather gloves she wore and offered them.

"Thank you, but the gravel might ruin them."

"Honey, I have more gloves. You need to protect your hands."

"Yes, ma'am." Emma knew the tone.

She needed to do what she was told by her smarter elder and more memories of her mother returned. It had been a while since anyone had given a thought to her well-being. Donning the gloves, she eased first one shoulder and then another through the opening. Once inside, she rose slowly, her eyes adjusting to the darkness. There were a few half-dollar size holes in the roof allowing shafts of light from the fading day to come through, but there were still shadows all over. A movement in the far corner caught her attention. She inched forward.

"Charlie… is that you? My name is Emma. Your grandmother needs you to come out now. It's really not very safe in here."

She heard a tiny whimper of an animal. Her eyes zoomed in on the area it came from. That was when she saw the small huddled figure on the ground next to an old couch with springs hanging out of the remnants of its cushions. The child looked up at her with wide eyes that immediately caught her attention. They were large in the pale face and a lighter silver gray color, but there was no mistaking she was related to the woman waiting outside. *Those eyes must run in the family.* Emma moved forward one step at a time. She stopped a couple feet from the child, trying not to intimidate or upset her. She lowered herself to rest on her knees, a smile of encouragement on her face.

"Is there a puppy under there you're worried about?"

The little girl nodded her head; moisture glistened in her eyes that remained on Emma.

"Well, if I try to get it out, will you go outside with your grandmother for me?"

Immediately, the head nodded up and down as the child

recognized the offer of help.

Emma held out her hand. "Take my hand and we'll get you to the door and then I'll come back for the puppy."

"Promise?" The child finally used her voice. It was small and hopefulness colored its tone.

"I promise."

Charlie stood and placed her small palm inside Emma's. She wanted to immediately gather her up and try to get her warmer, but it was best to move slowly and get her to her grandmother. In a couple of moments, she was at the small opening and helping Charlie crawl through to the other side. Once that was accomplished and the girl was in her grandmother's embrace, she turned back to the old couch.

Bending down, she had to practically lie down on her stomach amid all the litter and gravel and other things she didn't want to think about such as bugs and spiders and whatever else. She was grateful that the weather would preclude anything of a slithery reptile lying in wait and *that* she would definitely not tangle with. Taking out her cell phone, she shone the screen's light quickly so she could make out her objective.

The puppy was small. The head with one ear up and the other floppy and drooping downward seemed to be the largest part of its body. Slowly, she reached her hand out, trying not to frighten the animal any more than it already was and testing if it was going to come quietly with her. Touching one of its paws, she began stroking it slowly, her voice low and coaxing. Eventually, she was able to get a good grip on its front leg and she began to pull the dog toward her, while trying not to hurt him at the same time.

When the puppy finally emerged, she grasped him and sat back for a few moments to take a look at the creature that had caused so much trouble. It was definitely a stray. Tiny bones had a thin covering of skin and coarse brown and white hair stretched across it. He turned out to be a *she*. The large caramel brown eyes locked in her direction were huge with fear. There was a lot of white spriggy hair around her neck with a smattering of brown spots from her soft ears to the tip of her little tail. Her lineage was definitely "mutt".

"So, you're the troublemaker in all of this. There's someone waiting on you, little one. Let's go." Retracing her journey, she was soon outside the structure.

The storekeeper had joined the pair waiting on her.

"You got her! Can I hold her?" Charlie was already reaching arms towards the animal.

Emma glanced at the older woman for a moment and then, getting a head nod, she released the puppy to the child.

Immediately, the puppy was cradled inside the puffy purple material of the child's jacket. "You need to get warm. I'll get you warm."

"That's a scrawny little one." The storekeeper shook his head. "It was her and two others and the mother here for a couple of days. Saw them get dumped by a guy in a silver truck. He barely slowed down."

"I don't understand how people can be so cruel to helpless animals. Are the others around here?" The woman looked over at the man.

The slow shake of his head went along with a look in reply to her question that told Emma this little guy was probably the sole survivor of a bad situation. Her heart ached for the orphan... it was a kindred spirit of sorts.

"She needs a home, Grandma. We *have* to take her home." The little girl's eyes were wide with pleading and the pup seemed to be adding her own emphasis with soft cries at the same time. "She's cold and hungry and has no mommy... just like me."

Those words rang in the cold air and seemed to hang there for several moments. A sudden knot formed in the center of Emma's chest that made it hard to breathe.

"Charlie, you know your dad's rule about pets. He would be upset if we came home with a dog... much less a puppy that needs extra attention and care."

Charlie was on the verge of tears when she turned her eyes on Emma again. "Please... can you take her? She needs a home really bad. She's alone and scared. Please, *please* help her."

"Don't cry. I'll take her." *Have I lost my mind?* What possessed her to say those words? What was she going to do with a dog when the only roof she had over her head at the moment was a semi-functioning pickup loaded with all her worldly possessions? It was the little girl's tears that had done it. That and memories of how it felt to have her heart breaking over the loss of a treasured animal. She pushed the old memories away and took a deep breath. The past had no place in her present.

A small body was launched against her legs and one arm snaked around her waist while the child still tried to maintain control of the squirming pup. "Thank you, thank you, thank you. I know she'll be good for you. Do you live around here? I could come visit her maybe?"

Three pairs of eyes were trained on Emma in that moment. "Well, I… the fact is," she began but the older woman spoke up.

"Where's our manners, Charlie? We haven't even made introductions with this poor young lady." The woman stuck her hand out. "I'm Mae Drayton and this is my granddaughter, Charlene, as you already know." She looked at the man beside her.

"Jim Davies," he spoke up, extending his hand to Emma following Mae's example. "This is my store and all."

"It's nice to meet all of you. I'm Emma Cramer."

"And are you from this area?" Mae's question was a natural one.

"No… not really. I lived in Lassiter, a few miles from Frost Creek a long time ago. My mother died and I left the area. I'm just driving through… a little detour on my way to Dallas. I have a couple of job interviews there in the next few days. I only stopped here because my engine light came on and I was hoping to find a garage or mechanic, but Jim told me I have to drive on a piece to find one of those."

"I can't visit puppy?" Charlie's gray eyes clouded over again in her pale face.

"I'm sorry. I—"

"Charlie, the puppy has a good home now and you should be happy about that. And I owe you a good deal of thanks, Miss Cramer, for going after my granddaughter and rescuing both her and the pup."

"I'm glad I was able to help. I really should be going now since it's getting dark and the temperature is definitely dropping." She looked at the storekeeper. "Is the motel still open on the highway there in McKenna Springs? It's been a while since I've been through the area."

"Yes, it's still there."

"Then I best be on my way." Emma looked down at the child. "Would you like to carry her to my truck?" She received a quick nod in reply.

"I'll grab a box from the storeroom and some newspapers," Jim informed the trio and hustled toward the store.

Emma was self-conscious once they reached the truck. She saw Mae's eyes take in the scene of the few boxes in the back seat and a couple of battered suitcases and knew the woman saw more than what Emma wanted her to know. But Mae didn't make any comment. Emma remembered she still had on the gloves and quickly removed them, handing them toward the woman. "I'm sorry. I would have hated to go off with these. Thank you for loaning them to me."

Mae's smile was warm and reassuring and again, something tightened inside Emma's chest. "I'm glad our paths crossed, Miss Cramer."

"Please… it's Emma. And I'm glad also." And she meant it.

"You say you're on your way to Dallas for interviews. What sort of employment are you looking to find there?"

"I have my degree in office management with an emphasis on computer financial systems. I'm hoping to find employment at one of the banks. Two of them offered interviews this week. If not, I'm also experienced in hairstyling, waitressing, and short-order cooking if I have to fall back on something in the meantime." She tried to play it off as lightly as she could.

Jim arrived at that moment so she had no need to elaborate.

"This box should do and papers are inside it. And I added some canned food and a little pouch of dry food along with a water bottle, too. I'm sure that little one won't be choosy on what kind of meal she gets tonight."

Emma took the box and then went to reach inside her pocket, but Jim's hand raised in the air stopped her. "And no need of paying for nothing. That dog food doesn't sell all that fast so you're doing me a favor."

"I appreciate it, thank you." The time had come.

Emma sat the box inside the truck in the floorboard of

the front seat. She turned to Charlie, bending down to her level. She placed a reassuring smile on her face.

"I know this puppy will never forget the little girl who saved her. And, because you did, I think you should name her."

Charlie was up to the task. A wide grin split her elfin face with its smattering of freckles across the bridge of her nose.

Her eyes lit up. "She's Angel. The white circle around the brown on her head kind of looks like a halo like on the angel on your Christmas tree each year, right, Granny?"

"I do believe you're right." Mae nodded.

"Then Angel it is. Give her a big hug and let's put her in her box."

Charlie gave the pup a hug and whispered something in her ear. The grown-ups couldn't hear what it was. Then she reached over and set the pup inside the box. The pup stayed quiet during this new turn of events, mostly out of fear, Emma guessed as she shut the door.

"Well, goodbye, Charlie, and it was nice to meet all of you. Time for me to be on the road."

"Drive safely." Mae raised a hand in a small wave goodbye as Emma pulled away.

For a moment, Emma allowed herself a glance in the rearview mirror at the trio still standing watching her departure. There was no explaining the strange feeling that spread over her as the small scene disappeared behind her. She was leaving something behind her... something she hadn't felt in a very long time. For a moment, a sudden urge overtook her to turn around and go back. *Back to what?* She was tired and cold and that was why she was feeling strange. *Don't look back... never.* There was nothing for her there.

Chapter Two

CLOSED. BE BACK on Monday. Emma read the words a third time, but that didn't change them or the impact to her world. Of course, it was just her luck. The mechanic wasn't there. The gas station on the corner had closed an hour ago. There was a small liquor store across the highway with a couple of cars outside it. Three blocks down, she could see the sign of the small motel that had been there over fifteen years. Lights were just beginning to come on along the way even though darkness had come early with the impending cold front and its clouds blocking any sunset from the west.

Emma slid behind the steering wheel again and placed the truck into drive. There was a whining in the engine that hadn't been there except for the last couple of miles and it had her worried. It wouldn't be wise to try to make the additional ninety miles or so to Austin when there would be nothing for most of those miles but ranchland and few inhabitants. She pulled the vehicle back onto the highway, passed a couple more closed buildings, and then turned into the parking lot of the motel. Her heart sank when her eyes caught the blinking red letters of the "No Vacancy" sign in the window. By the number of vehicles, mostly oilfield trucks and such, she could guess the sign was correct.

Since the oil boom had surfaced again in that part of the state, hotels rooms and any other places to stay had become a premium. That was another thing that was in the back of her mind… her budget. She had counted in the motel room she would need in the city but not for any along the way caused by the sudden need for car repairs or other detours. There was a soft whine from the floorboard area beside her and she caught sight of the fact the puppy had decided to wake up and check out the situation. She sounded as forlorn as Emma was feeling inside.

"I totally agree, Angel. Guess I'll think positive and go inside and see if there is any hope like a cancellation or something." Here she was talking to an animal like she expected her to understand and even engage in conversation with her. "What am I doing with you? I can barely take care of myself right now let alone a dog. Sorry you got stuck with me, little one. Maybe I can find you a better home once we get to the city."

Her mind went back to the woman and the little girl. They had been nice and the woman reminded her more than once of her mother… before life had gotten her too far down to bounce back any longer. Mae Drayton had a far different life than her mom had endured. She liked to think her mother would have looked like Mae had circumstances been different. *Silly thoughts.* Yet, she had been drawn to the woman. And also to little Charlie. When she had made mention of the fact she had no mother, that had kicked Emma in the gut. Poor child already had experienced a hard blow in life. Emma sent a quick little prayer into the growing darkness that Charlie would find someone to be her mother soon. Anyone would love to have a cutie like her for their own. Until then, maybe that guardian angel, like in Emma's childhood photo, would look over her.

Maybe someday... *maybe...* she might be lucky enough to have such a child. And someone to care for her... to not be alone. *Maybe.* But then she would just be better off taking care of herself. It only led to heartbreak when she let someone else... or *something...* and her eyes fell on the little pup... into her life. *Keep it simple. Rely only on yourself.* That was her motto she had decided a while back. She'd only get in trouble if she forgot it.

Emma found the sign was indeed correct and there would be no rooms available for a few weeks. Things were looking bleaker by the minute. Driving into the heart of the town, the bright neon sign of The Diner on Main Street lured her toward it. Things might look better with a sandwich and something warm to drink. She needed to formulate her next moves with care. As she drove the last block, a strange clanking noise began somewhere underneath her truck. It wasn't loud, but her ears picked up on it in a heartbeat. *Please, not now. Why can't you just let me get to*

Dallas?

The bright smile of the waitress was too much for Emma to match as she took the menu from her. The sinking feeling inside her was settling in and things looked more than a little hopeless. She needed her pickup to make it another hundred miles. Reality told her that would not be the case. She had heard that clanking sound once before in her mother's old sedan. They had to let it rust behind their trailer because they never could gather the over three thousand dollars needed to replace the transmission and other parts. What was she going to do?

"My, my... that sad face doesn't look like the one I left not too long ago." The words brought her out of her pity party and up to see Mae Drayton standing next to the booth, a worried look of concern in the soft gray eyes. "You look like you might have lost your last friend."

"I'm sorry." Emma summoned a halfhearted smile. "I guess I was deep in thought." Shaking her head, she widened her smile. "It's a nice surprise to see you again."

"I dropped Charlie off at her Sunday school's slumber party and thought I'd take a quick detour by here to pick up one of Darcy's cobblers to take home." She stood waiting with a calming smile on her face.

Emma nodded at the empty space across from her. "If you'd like to sit while you're waiting?"

The woman didn't hesitate but slid into the booth, loosening the scarf from around her neck and removing her gloves. She gave the waitress a broad smile as she approached.

"I'll have a coffee, Maggie. And let's have a couple of the specials for today." Her gaze swung over to Emma. "You've got to try some of that cobbler, but you need something more substantial in your stomach before you have that sugar." She gave a laugh and ignored Emma's attempt to wave off the offer of food. "I hate eating alone and there's no one home tonight so it would be a waste for me to cook for just myself. Looks like I need your help once again this evening."

Both Mae and the waitress looked at her then and Emma had a feeling that Mae was a woman who rarely had anyone disagree with any of her plans. She had to admit it would be nice to taste one of those grilled ham sandwiches and bowl of tomato soup that had been coming out of the kitchen to the other patrons. "I suppose I could try—"

Mae didn't let her finish before she sent the waitress to the back with their order. "This diner has the best home-cooking of anyplace… with the exception of your own home. I've fooled my family with it a time or two when I didn't feel like cooking at my own stove." Mae had a delightful soft laugh. "Now, suppose you tell me why you looked like you had the weight of the world on those slender shoulders when I arrived?" She changed the subject so fast; Emma was caught off guard.

"It's… just some truck issues and the mechanic is indeed not available for a couple of days. Mr. Davies was correct."

"Truck issues as in something major, right? Expensive probably and there goes the budget." Mae summed it up in a nutshell. "I remember those days too well. Seemed every time we were about to see the light of day, some piece of equipment or a vehicle would break down and there we would be broke again. Can't say how many times I just wanted to throw in the towel and move back home with my family."

"Why didn't you?"

"Well, I had my husband and two baby sons who needed me to stay strong for them. I came from tough Oklahoma stock and we didn't give up at the first sign of trouble... or the second or third." She finished it with a laugh. "I married a tough Texan, too. So, we kept putting our faith in the good Lord and moving forward as best we could." Her eyes grew softer as memories shared the moment. "While those were very tough times and I wouldn't want to live through them again, they were still some of the best. They got us to where we are today. Makes us appreciate what we have all the more." Her gaze landed on Emma. "Enough about me and mine, what can we do about your problem?"

"I just have to figure out how to get my truck repaired and get to Dallas. I'll probably miss my interview opportunity, but I have to hope there'll be something else I can apply for. If all else fails, I can fall back on one of my other experiences until I get my funds built up again to move on down the road."

"Move on down the road…" Mae's voice trailed off as their food arrived. She didn't speak again until the waitress had left them and they had each taken a few bites of food. "Sounds like you really would prefer to have a job where your computer and other skills might be put to use instead of standing on your feet all day doing hair or waiting on tables. Am I right?"

Emma nodded her head. "That's why I worked hard to get through school and all. To take a few steps up that imaginary ladder. But sometimes you have to do what you need to do and not what you want."

Mae leaned back in the booth, her gaze calm and assessing as it encompassed Emma. "I'm a pretty good judge of character and, from what I've seen already, I think you'll land on your feet. And I think I have a business proposition that might just help you out… and my family, too. But I want you to understand that it is strictly business and not in the least related to a handout of any sort. It's a tough job with a boss that, well, needs to be reminded he's part of the human race again… but we'll leave that detail for right now. You open to hearing my offer out?"

Emma was a little intrigued and she appreciated the forthright manner that Mae had of putting things. What else did she have to do with her time in that moment? "I'm always willing to listen."

"Good girl." Mae leaned forward, moving her plate and coffee cup to the side. She settled in and began to speak in a matter of fact way, laying out the details. "Our family has some land just west of here. Over the years, it's grown into a bigger business than we could have hoped and we are grateful for that. Three years ago, we shifted some of the business… my husband, Vernon, still maintains the farming side of things. Our son, Cole, branched out and maintains the ranching side of our affairs. He's Charlie's father. And he is why I need *you*." She paused for a moment, taking a sip from her water glass. "Actually, we *all* need you… each in our own ways. But it's paramount that I find someone who can get my son's office into the first semblance of order it's ever seen. He's not only having to maintain the cattle part of the business, but he is also the interim sheriff in this county after our regular sheriff was hurt in a bad traffic accident.

"The secondary reason we need you… is Charlie. She's talked of little else since you left us at that station. She's usually more reserved with people—almost to the point of shyness. I usually take the majority of care of her during the day, and sometimes the evenings, too, since… well, since her mother left us when Charlie was less than a year old. I'm not a spring chicken any longer and, as you saw today, I can't quite keep up with a precocious five-year old as I once could. To sum up, I want to offer you a job that is two-fold.

"You'll be getting my son's business affairs in order using your computer skills. At the same time, you'll be helping me out by being the younger person in my granddaughter's life. She goes to her kinder class during the day so she's out of your way while you have your office work. Of course, you'll have a comfortable living arrangement on the ranch, a benefit plan, and your salary will be adequate."

The sum she added was indeed adequate and then some. Emma was in mild shock and struggled to get her brain and speech in sync. To make that much salary and then have the major living expenses included too... it was almost too much to believe how her luck could change in the space of a few hours. That would enable her to save faster than she could any other way. Not even a half hour before she was at her wit's end on how she would overcome the latest setbacks in her life and then Mae arrived like some guardian angel out of the blue. Now she was being handed an unbelievable opportunity. "My only experience with children is the little I was with them in a church daycare setting. And then I mostly took care of the babies in the nursery."

"I've seen you with Charlie. And you can't fool a child. She likes you already. I trust my instinct and I think you're a natural... you just have to be yourself. It certainly wouldn't hurt you to be able to put aside a good nest egg, maybe have enough to get a more dependable vehicle, and, if you find you want to move on after say, six months or so... then you'll have a good recommendation in your pocket and the savings to take you where you want to go. What other offer do you have to beat this one?"

THOSE WORDS HAD echoed in her mind more than once since they left the diner and now she pulled her truck into the circular driveway in front of a large, one-story brick home that was long and rambling, set on the sloping rise of a slight hill about fifteen minutes from town. By the number of outlying barns and workshop-type buildings situated a little distance down the slope of the hill, she had a fairly good impression that this was one of those prosperous farms and not just a simple, small, family-run operation as she first pictured in her mind.

"Well, Angel, it's a job… for the time being. And they allow dogs at this house which is a good thing." Especially since these were the people who saddled her with the pup to begin with. And Emma could put up with anything that would get her down the road toward that new life.

Stepping inside the front door of the house was instantly welcoming. It was warm and there was an aroma of something freshly baked coming from wherever the kitchen might be. The furnishings were tasteful and "country-charming" as her mother labeled the photographs in the magazines she used to collect and stare at over and over until they literally fell apart. *Someday…* they would have such a house with furniture and pretty things she would say, pointing to the photos and reminding her daughter of how the future would change for them. When her mother died, Emma had taken the box with the clippings and tossed them in the trash barrel. It was ironic that she now found herself in that world… if only for a brief time.

"Come in and make yourself at home," Mae called as she hung her coat in the hall closet and then moved into the living room, switching on another lamp as she went. "We have a mud room off the kitchen that we can make little Angel a bed in and get her fed and settled in for the night. The floor is tiled so if she has any accidents not on the paper, it won't be a problem."

Emma followed her down another hall and into a large, brick and wood-beamed kitchen that was another page out of a magazine. The mudroom was a good size and Mae opened a closet and took out a basket. "I have an old blanket in here too," she said, rummaging around. "Here it is. And I'll get a couple of bowls for her. The backyard is fenced so if you want to take her out for a couple of minutes, I'll get things settled in here."

Emma took the pup outside and the wind was even more brisk than a few minutes ago. She sat the dog down on the green grass and stuck her hands inside her pants' pockets for warmth. She needed to find some gloves for herself when she was next in town. "Hurry, Angel. This isn't time to explore. It's dark and too cold." It seemed Angel was of the same mind.

The pup did what it needed to do and returned to Emma quickly enough. She scooped her up and stepped back into the warmth of the house.

"I've got her food and water dishes ready and her bed,

too. She might cry a bit in her new surroundings but being back here, she won't keep us awake."

Emma sat the pup in her bed and stepped to join Mae in the doorway. "Goodnight, little Angel, sweet dreams."

Mae closed the door behind them. "If you want to bring in your suitcase, we'll get you settled next."

Emma made a quick trip out to her truck and retrieved her purse and the suitcase. Anything else could wait until the morning when she knew exactly where she might be ending up. Back inside the house, she followed Mae's voice to find her down another hallway and inside a bedroom that was done in blues and greens and was the nicest room Emma had ever stayed in with its fluffy, quilted covers on the double bed and the matching ruffled curtains at the window. The floor was carpeted in a soft cream and welcomed one to take off their shoes and enjoy.

"You have a bathroom through that door, and the closet is here," Mae said, opening the sliding door and revealing the space with plenty of hangars… more than Emma would use. "If you can think of anything else you need, you just let me know. Our room is at the opposite end of the house. Vernon won't be in for another couple of hours or so. He and my son are at the cattlemen's meeting tonight so that could go on and on. You'll meet him tomorrow. My son will be a little harder to pin down, but we'll get you both together soon enough. Now, you just make yourself at home, and sleep until you wake up tomorrow. Travel always tires me out so I expect you can use some rest before Charlie has to be collected in the afternoon."

Emma didn't waste much time taking a hot bath and getting rid of the travel dust and letting her worries temporarily evaporate with the steam forming from the heated water. For the way the day had started and had gone downhill, things had certainly turned around in a surprising way. Toweling dry, she slipped into a pair of sleep shorts and a tank top. She actually found herself relaxing for the first time in a long while as she cuddled down under the quilted covers, turned onto her side, and allowed a long sigh to escape her. Once the lamp was turned off, the room was in total darkness and she snuggled under the warmth of quilts. Whatever tomorrow would bring, it could wait for the moment. In no time at all, her eyes grew heavier and soon closed and bad dreams stayed away as she fell into a deeper sleep than she had experienced in a very long time.

"YOU KNOW WHERE your room is," Vernon Drayton said over his shoulder to his son as they entered the house. "You need something more to eat, like a sandwich, you know where the refrigerator is. Just clean up so your mom won't have either of our heads. I'll see you in the morning."

"Thanks, Dad. I'm beat. I just need that pillow. See you at breakfast."

Cole moved down the hall on autopilot. He didn't need to bother with lights. He had been born and raised inside the walls of this house and knew it like the back of his hand. He stepped into the bedroom, careful to not make noise out of habit. When he came in late from work, it was second nature to try not to disturb his sleeping daughter. He stripped his clothes in nothing flat, mindful to at least make sure they hit the bench at the end of the bed and not the floor. He moved around the edge and then pulled back the cover, sliding his long body onto the cool sheets.

As usual habit, he turned on his side and his arm reached to bunch the pillow next to him. Only the pillow wasn't there… something else that took a second to recognize was. And, when it registered in his brain he wasn't alone in bed and he was cupping the curves of a female, that was also the same time there was a swift movement in the bed next to him and all hell broke loose. He tried to break his fall as his body received a blow that sent him reaching out in the dark to try and lessen the impact with the floor.

His loud curses mingled with a shriek from the person jumping from the bed on the opposite side. The bright light illuminated the room just as Cole rose from the floor and faced the other shocked occupant.

"What the hell are you doing in here!"

"Who are you?"

THEY SPOKE IN unison and then both fell silent... in shock. Emma realized two things in no particular order... one was the fact she was standing in front of a strange man dressed in her scanty attire. The second was the fact the man, whoever he was, was standing facing her with nothing on but a pair of white briefs that left very little to one's imagination given the way they molded to his lower body. In a different circumstance, she might have stood in gaping awe of how hard muscled and perfectly proportioned he was... in more ways than one. The thought brought crimson heat to her face... and a heat to other parts of her body that should be ignored as fast as possible.

His gaze was taking its own inventory of her too, and the only thing that brought them both out of their shocked stances was the sound of Mae's voice coming down the hall. In a lightning move, the man grabbed the top throw off the foot of the bed and wrapped it around his middle just as Mae arrived in the doorway, followed by a tall, older man in striped pajamas. Emma grabbed the shirt from the bench beside her and held it up in front of her undressed state. It was the best she could do in the amount of time she had.

"Whatever happened in here?" Mae looked from Emma to the man and back again. She looked to be not shocked but almost pleased in some way. "I see you two have met."

"I have no idea who this woman is." He lost no time in setting his mother straight.

"Well, I certainly don't know who *you* are or why you

attacked me in my bed." Emma had no problem setting him straight either.

"Attacked you? Are you crazy? And that is *not* your bed. It used to be mine… and still *is,* I thought."

"I think we should begin by meeting each other." Mae took control. "Emma, may I present my son and Charlie's father, Cole Drayton." She smiled at her son. "Cole, this is Emma Cramer, the woman I hired today to get your life in order. It's late and we all need our sleep. Let's get back to bed and leave the rest for the morning. Cole, you can sleep in the bedroom across the hall. I can see you two are going to get along just fine… just fine, indeed."

Chapter Three

O**NCE THE DOOR** clicked shut behind his parents, Cole spoke first.

"I obviously will discuss this whole idea of a job offer with my mother in the morning." The man's tone matched the scowl on his face... a face that might be termed handsome if his attitude didn't belie that fact. Emma didn't care for the attitude or for his suggestion of speaking to anyone *about her* without *her* involved.

She should have known it was all too good to be true. "And it's obvious that it wouldn't work anyway."

His frown deepened as his gaze narrowed on her. "Obvious? You think so? Why?"

"It's clear you aren't in favor of the idea of having anyone help you out in your office or with your daughter. To have someone forced upon you wouldn't make for a conducive working environment. It works better for everyone to be able to be pleasant and have some enjoyment in their work. It makes for better productivity." It was difficult to be as professional in her delivery as she would have liked, but they didn't teach her in her business classes how to face a prospective employer in a bedroom, not an office, and when they were both dressed in very little clothing... and he had just copped a feel of her breast.

"Pretty speech there. And how do you know I'm not a pleasant person to work for?"

An eyebrow rose as she landed her blue-eyed gaze on him. "I base it on the last few minutes in your company. You know nothing of my abilities, you obviously don't value your mother's opinion of my qualifications, and you've stated you intend to tell her that I am not hired. Did I leave anything out?"

His grip brought the coverlet draped around his waist to a tighter fit as he moved slowly around the end of the bed and did not stop until he was within a foot of where she stood. He was tall and she had to look up. Which was a good thing in one way... her eyes had something to latch on to besides the broad expanse of a naked chest with its light smattering of golden brown hair that fell into a "V" that disappeared under the folds of the cloth at his waist. Her fingers curled as she shook her mind away from a sudden urge to reach out and test how soft those fine *hairs* might be. *Concentrate!*

"I think any discussion on this topic can wait until the morning. So, let's trade."

"Trade?" What was he talking about?

The silver gray eyes fell to the shirt she still clutched in front of her chest. "My shirt for this wrap. On the count of three. And I promise not to look... if you do the same."

Was that a hint of sarcasm in that glint that appeared in his eyes as he spoke the words? Well, if he was trying to rattle her, he was going to come up short.

"One, two, three." She held out the shirt, her eyes locked with his. Emma determined to keep an even smile on her face.

He took his time, a hint of a smile turning up the corner of his mouth, a *taunting* hint. The material was slowly unwrapped.

Emma was determined to not let him see he was undermining her control. The shirt remained hooked on the finger of the hand still in the space between them.

Finally, the cover was held out toward her and her free hand grabbed it, bringing it against her front. He reached for the shirt but not nearly as fast. And, when he did take it off her finger, he didn't do anything but smile.

"Thanks. You have sweet dreams." He sauntered out of the room and Emma counted to twenty and resisted the urge to turn and take a peek. When the door latched behind him, she exhaled the breath she had been holding. Great first and *last* impression. Now she needed to come up with plan B as she just lost her job before she ever got started. *Too bad the son wasn't as nice as his mother.* Maybe he was adopted!

WAY TO GO in not listening to me, Mother. Cole turned once again and punched the pillow before balling it under his head. He was having a devil of a time getting comfortable. Something else he was ready to blame on the woman across the hall, who was sleeping in *his* bed to which she had no right to do. This was what happened when his mother wouldn't listen to what he said and believe he meant it.

Maybe he *had* told her he could use someone with computer skills for his office. But that was all… and he was only saying the words to make a hasty exit from the whole subject in general. He had landed in another mess.

He turned on his back and stared up at the ceiling above the bed, his arms locking above his head. Sleep wasn't coming anytime soon. His mind wouldn't shut down. It was the same subject as many other nights. What could he do? He was trying to make everyone happy and do what was expected of him. He knew what his mother had said that day was right. It was just as right all the other times she had brought up the subject.

Charlie needed a woman's touch and a home that was more than just a house. *He knew that.* But the problem was, he wasn't about to risk any more disappointment or pain… certainly nothing that might touch his daughter. She had been too young when his ex-wife had deserted them. He was grateful for that. And he was determined not to place her in any situation where someone else could inflict the same harm again. And now it just got harder with the advent of the woman across the hall.

How was he supposed to know she was in that room? He did what he had done many nights before when he had gone to meetings with his dad and Charlie was on an overnight. He went on autopilot, shedding his clothing, and crawling under the covers. Only tonight when he reached for the pillow next to him, he had encountered a female breast… a very nice, firm one as his memory brought the moment back in Technicolor. That caused another sensation to warm his body. One that had become somewhat of a stranger in recent months. Even then, just the memory caused him to kick the covers off his body, seeking cooler temperatures.

When the lights had come on, and he had picked himself up off the floor, he had glimpsed the rest of a very nicely shaped body that disappeared from view in seconds behind his shirt. That was when his gaze took in the rest of the woman in front of him. She had long chestnut-colored hair that fell thick around her shoulders and down her back. Brilliant, large blue eyes blazed at him in a face that held his attention longer than he wanted to admit, his gaze noting the mouth with the fuller bottom lip that she seemed to have a habit of running a sliver of her pink tongue over in a nervous gesture. The movement had also caught his attention more than once.

He admitted it. Cole had snuck more than a couple of glances at the tanned length of leg that the shirt didn't conceal. *Not bad.* And then she had spoken and that pretty much put an end to his perusal of her assets. She was a woman who had no problem standing her ground. That had caught him off guard. He had to admit while it aggravated him, it also intrigued him. She wasn't mean, just forthright in stating facts. She had a brain… and a body. And those reasons together made her an even worse choice for his household.

Well, whatever his mother had promised her, she could just forget it. He would have a word with Mae in the morning and then she could send Miss Emma whatever-her-last-name-was packing. And his life would continue just fine. He punched the pillow again to emphasize his point. The covers came back over his legs.

"Before you begin, I will speak." Mae was ahead of her son who came into the kitchen just as she was pouring a cup of coffee. She pushed it in front of him as he slid into one of the chairs at the table. "You said I needed to find you someone to straighten out your office and I did just that. The fact that she and Charlie hit it off so well, is just an added plus."

Cole halted the mug half way to his mouth, his gaze locking on his mother's. "Charlie? How did she meet Charlie?"

"She rescued your daughter from that old, dilapidated

garage behind Jim Davies' store yesterday. Charlie had followed a stray pup inside and I couldn't get through the opening to get her. Emma came along and went right in after her. Charlie took to her like I've not seen her do with a stranger before. She was so sad when Emma had to leave."

"And that would be far worse when she leaves from the job after being in it for a while. No girl like her is going to be content on a ranch in the middle of nowhere. She wouldn't stick it out long. Charlie doesn't need heartbreak and people moving in and out of her life."

"Emma agreed to at least six months. And we even shook hands on it. She was on her way to Dallas with a couple of job interviews lined up when she had engine trouble. It sounds serious. And this works out well because she can build up her funds, fix the truck, and then be on her way. You know I've always been a good judge of character and I believe she's the type to keep her word once she gives it.

"Get over it, Cole. I offered her the job you gave me permission to fill. There's got to be something else going on here for you to have this sort of attitude toward making any changes in your life. What's going on? And putting on your 'considering look' doesn't work on me."

The woman was watching him with that eagle eye of hers and he took a long sip of his coffee. Something told him that she wasn't going to give up on the subject. And she was getting too close to a topic he didn't want her near.

"Nothing else is going on." He leaned back in his chair, arms folded over his chest. He axed his *considering look*. "If you offered the job and she accepted, and you made clear what her responsibilities would be, then I suppose it's best to get this over. I'll go along with the six months. But this is the *end* of your interfering in the running of my household and my life. You've got to let me handle things my way for Charlie and me. Agreed?"

Mae bestowed a wide smile on her son. "As you say. I'm sure you'll be happy with my choice. And you will thank me in six months."

"Don't get carried away. And who knows? She might have changed her mind after last night. She might not want to stick around. Whenever she gets out of bed, you might ask her."

"I already did. And she agrees to much the same as you just did."

"*Already did?* You mean she's up?" That brought his attention to alert.

"She was up and having coffee with your father when I finally came in... about five-thirty this morning. She went with him down to the garage and then he was probably going to show off the barns. I told them not to be late for breakfast. Which I better get going right now." She stood and began moving pans and utensils around the cabinet and stove.

She was humming, too, obviously pleased about something. Cole wasn't going to ask what it was. He had an idea he had just been played by a master.

No one was in the first barn that he checked. Cole moved on to the garage where the larger machinery was kept while being worked on. That was where he found the pair. He stopped, hands on hips, giving himself a moment or two to take in what he was seeing.

Only his father's legs were visible from beneath the farm truck that usually hauled bales of hay to the different fields for the animals. The hood was up and there was a shapely figure of a female dressed in denim jeans and red and black top draped over the side fender, her feet balanced on a step stool while the top half of her was somewhere inside the engine compartment.

"That's the way." His father's voice drifted within his hearing. "You hold that lug nut tight with those pliers and I'll just fit the top on and screw into place. That'll just about fix her right up."

Emma went up on tiptoe, the stool giving just a slight wobble, and Cole made his move. He slid one arm unceremoniously around the trim waist and lifted the woman off the stool and out of his way. It was a move she didn't take too kindly towards him making.

"Quit the kicking and squirming," he ordered, moving her off to the side and setting her feet on the ground. He turned his attention to the engine compartment. Retrieving the pliers from her fingers, he bent over and secured the nut.

"Go ahead, Dad."

"Got it." The man slid out from underneath the truck, using the hand his son shot out to him to pull himself to his feet. "Emma and I had already done all the others, don't know why you showed up to do *one*." He shot the girl a broad grin. "My son don't treat you right over at his place, you come back here and I'll hire you right on the spot. You have the makings of a good farmhand."

"Based on what? She held a pair of pliers steady?" Something about his father's words of praise irked Cole on top of everything else the woman had put him through the last few sleepless hours.

His father gave him a long look. "Get another cup of coffee and better manners to go along with it. I'll be up at the house getting my breakfast. You put away the tools and then apologize to Emma, as you escort her nicely to breakfast."

Cole didn't respond. He looked at where Emma stood, arms crossed over her plaid shirt, her hair braided in a long braid which she flipped over her shoulder. Her blue eyes were just as brilliant in the morning light and they spoke volumes, and he would wager that none of them were nice words.

"Maybe I should have used a bit more finesse, but it wasn't safe being on the edge of that stool. You could have been hurt."

She simply stood watching him, no response. Was she giving him the silent treatment or something?

"I apologized."

"Your father and I were doing just fine. I doubt falling off a two-foot stool would have seriously injured anyone. I'm a lot tougher than you might think. I was glad to be able to help *him*. He's been very kind and I appreciate his niceness." She turned on her heel and left him.

"Niceness? What kind of word is that?" He received no response.

She continued on her way toward the house. It didn't help his attitude any when he caught himself watching her departure in the way a male enjoyed watching a beautiful woman in a form-fitting pair of jeans walk... *Hold on!* Since when had he spent time ogling any female's figure? *A long, long time.* That fact didn't make his disposition any sunnier. Emma Cramer was trouble. He didn't know how he knew it, but he knew it just the same. Six months... and not one minute more! He couldn't wait for that day.

"Have another biscuit, Emma. Don't be shy around our table. I married the best cook in the state, as the size of my waistline can attest." Vernon passed the plate to Emma with a grin. "And try both the bacon and the sausage. Can't find any better tasting pork. You have plenty of scrambled eggs?"

"Just in case anyone cares, I would like another biscuit and some more eggs, too." Cole watched the interactions of his parents with Emma and felt more unease. Things were settling around him at a speed he couldn't seem to slow down.

"Don't be silly, Cole. We don't get to spoil too many guests around here, so we're making up for it. You can certainly help yourself with no problems." His mother smiled her reply across the table.

"Guest? Since when is an employee a guest? Or did she already change her mind and will be leaving us... after breakfast, of course."

"*She* did not change her mind. But you are correct on one thing. I'm not a guest and as such, I fully expect to help with the cleanup." She met his gaze with her own.

Cole opened his mouth to make a comeback, but a sound caught his attention. He turned in that direction. "What was that? Is something in the laundry room? That sounded like an animal."

Vernon just raised his brow a bit and continued to study the food on his plate. He left it to his wife to supply the answer.

"Sounded like one because it *is* one. Remember I told you about how Charlie ran into that dilapidated garage after a stray puppy? And how Emma crawled in and rescued them both? Well, Emma was also kind enough to give the puppy a home at Charlie's pleading." Her smile grew broader as she beamed it on her son. "Guess that means little Angel will be living at Charlie's home after all. Isn't it grand how things work out? Charlie fell in love with that little one."

"Just *grand*. But that dog will be leaving when its owner leaves. Then Charlie will be upset. I believe the dog should stay here. Best solution." He didn't expect anyone to counter that edict as he rose and grabbed his hat off the back corner of his chair, sliding it on his head.

"You aren't leaving yet?" Mae asked as he stopped at her chair and dropped a swift kiss on her forehead. "Emma's not quite finished. You'll want to take her to your place so she can settle in and all."

"Sorry. I have a meeting with the county judge. Guess *you'll* have to settle her in and all." He tossed a look at the woman sitting quietly and watching him with her eloquent blue eyes.

While her demeanor and words might be polite enough for an employee, her eyes could certainly send a different signal. Well, he was the boss and she would soon find out what his rules would be in *his* house.

He kept the grin off his face until he cleared the room and was headed toward his vehicle parked in the drive. Served those two scheming females right. He had work to do and wasn't the welcome wagon. Besides, Emma Cramer coming to his home was not *his* idea. The less interaction with the irritating Miss Cramer, the better he would like it. And she need not think he would be treating her as a *guest* in his house. She had her place and that was how it would be. In his house, his rules were the law... same as in his county.

Chapter Four

"Believe it or not, I did raise my son to have better manners. He's got a lot of pressure on him right now and all. And... well, the situation with Charlie's mother may have colored a lot of things over the years, too. I hope you won't take anything he says to heart. You just stand your ground and give it right back to him." Mae led the way up the walk toward the three-story home that was to be Emma's residence for the next six months. Emma tried to pay attention to what Mae was saying, but her gaze was taking in everything else.

Cole and Charlie's home was something out of one of her childhood dreams. It was a Victorian-styled farmhouse from decades gone by. The wide porch ran across the front and down the sides. Larger-than-usual-sized windows were probably the norm in order to take advantage of the unfettered breezes. There was an understated country elegance about it and she had to smile. Her mother would have loved it. Emma would have given anything to have had such a place growing up.

Yet, there was something about it that wasn't right. The

yard needed some tending. The flower beds were plentiful, but with overgrowth and a few scraggly bushes here and there that were trying to hang on. It just seemed to need attention and a little loving care. Evidently, Cole Drayton didn't possess a green thumb. But then, he was a busy man. Mae had said as much. Emma decided she could cut him some slack in that regard.

The inside of the house was well laid out. The rooms were large with high ceilings and the old woodwork was intricate from the wooden floors to the scrollwork of the arched doorways. The furnishings were sturdy and ample. But it lacked color. And the small touches one would find that people collected over the years… were minimum. There were photos on the mantelpiece… mostly of Charlie as a baby and one of Mae and Vernon. But no sign of the brother she had heard mentioned only once by Mae. She saw nothing of any woman who might be Charlie's mother. Perhaps it was too sad for him? Had it been a recent loss? She would like to know more, but didn't feel comfortable enough to bring up the subject.

Mae reached the second floor ahead of her. "Up here, you have the master bedroom with a bath attached on the left. Down the hallway here, you have Charlie's room. Your room is across the hall from hers. I've tried to keep things dusted as best I can, but I don't guarantee it." She pushed open the door and allowed Emma to enter first.

"I love the big windows. It must be wonderful up here in

the spring with the cool breezes blowing through." Emma looked out over the scene of the front yard and the long road leading to the house.

She surveyed the rest of the room. There was a double bed, nightstand, dresser with mirror over it. The walls were off white and the bedspread and curtains were a soft blue.

"There's a large closet and you share the bathroom off the hallway with Charlie. Sorry about the plastic bath toys in the tub. There are plenty of linens and towels in the linen closet at the end of the hallway. Let's check out the kitchen and pantry."

The kitchen was large, too. "This is amazing. So many cabinets and the island is immense."

Mae smiled. "I like the fact you can appreciate the beauty of this old gal. She was built in the late 1930s by Vernon's dad. He left it in his will to Cole."

"This has the feel a home should have. Plus, it has history to it. You're lucky to have that."

"Not too many young people these days like old things like this. You have taste and a sense of history. I knew you were a special young lady when I met you." Mae walked over and slid back the barn door that had the walk-in pantry behind it. "It's fairly stocked with basics. You shop at Murphy's and your name will be on the account by this afternoon. We use the pharmacy next door and you'll do the same there. I made a list for you of other stores where you can use Cole's account. McKenna Springs is easy to navigate.

Did you ever visit here when you lived in Frost Creek?"

"A few times, but it was a long time ago. It should be fine."

Mae stepped through another doorway and on one side was a mudroom leading to a back door. The other side opened onto a covered screened-in porch. "I see by your smile that this meets with your approval. If you like this area, you'll love the sunroom on the other side of the house. That's great in the fall and winter months. It even has a fireplace at one end. I don't think it's ever been used by Cole, but it's there."

"Now, I have a list also that covers Charlie's schedule and school and all." Mae brought them back into the kitchen and to the long island with its bar stools along one side. She opened her bag and laid a tablet in front of Emma. "I tried to jot down everything I could think of about Charlie on there for you. And there's also a couple things about Cole, too. I know my son isn't the most communicative person in the world when he gets in a mood, so I hope it helps."

"You're amazing. When did you do all this?" Emma looked at the several pages covered in all sorts of information.

"This morning while I was cooking breakfast. I have always been a list-maker."

"I didn't see an office. Where do I work on the files for the cattle business?"

Mae nodded her head. "This way, and I apologize for the

mess you're about to see. Cole tells me he knows where everything is, but I doubt it. I just keep the doors shut and try to not go in there when I'm here."

Retracing their steps to the front door, they came to a set of double doors just off to the right in a recessed alcove. Mae hesitated and gave a glance to Emma. "Promise you won't turn and run in the opposite direction?"

"If I was going to do that, I would have done it the moment I met your son." Emma stopped as she caught what she had blurted out. "I'm sorry. That didn't come out right. I don't mean—"

"That's why I know you're perfect for this job." Mae shook her head and smiled. "You'll not let him bully you and you'll give as well as you get. Being the sheriff and all, he's used to people doing what he says and no one giving him any backtalk. But he needs to be brought down to earth now and then. I trust you to do that whenever needed."

"Yes, but he *is* my boss. I was trained to—"

"Nonsense... *I'm* your boss. *I* hired you. He can't fire you, only I can do that. Unless this runs you off first." With that, she slid the double doors wide and stepped aside for Emma to take in the sight before her.

Sight was the word for it. Emma looked slowly around the room. It was large. It had to be to hold all the filing cabinets and tables and the huge desk that had to be buried under a mountain of files and papers and trade magazines. She saw the top of a computer terminal on the desk also.

"Oh my..."

"Oh my, indeed. You've got your work cut out for you in here." Mae shook her head.

"Well, I will try to do my best. I never promised to be a miracle worker."

"It's best to just shut these doors and walk away. Besides, we need to get into town and pick up Charlie at the school. She's going to be so surprised and so happy."

Mae stopped on the porch after she closed the door behind them. She handed a key ring to Emma. "There's a house key. And one to the storage barn in the back. Another one for the pickup that's in the garage. You should use it whenever you run errands. There are gas pumps on the other side of the barn that you can use to fill up. You need to consider this your home while you're here, Emma. If there is something you need and you can't find it, call me. You have my number and Vernon's in your cell from this morning. I can be here in ten minutes if need be and those pesky deputies stay out of my way. In an emergency, you type in 321 and we all know to come running." They shared a laugh down the sidewalk.

"What about Angel? I really can't expect you all to keep her at your place."

"Vernon is sending a couple of hands over this afternoon. I wouldn't be surprised if they arrive while we're gone and get that taken care of even before Charlie gets home. They're putting up a fence at the back where those lovely huge pecan trees are, just off the back door."

"I thought Cole had a rule about no pets?"

"That's nonsense. Cole had dogs growing up. It was only—" Mae stopped her train of thought. Emma noted the frown that came and went before Mae picked up the thread again, her tone even. "He just doesn't have the time to bother with them. But he won't have to with you and Charlie handling things. So, don't worry about that."

Emma didn't push the matter but she couldn't help wondering what Mae had been about to say before she caught herself.

The drive into McKenna Springs was a pleasant one. Mae kept up a running commentary of the town, their neighbors, and a variety of other tidbits. She slowed the car when they approached the tall, stately courthouse set in the middle of a grove of oak and pecan trees on a grassy square in the center of the town. She managed to find a spot to park and Emma followed her exit from the car. Things seemed to be busy around the shops and square and Emma took note of some stores she might like to visit when next she had the opportunity. While she had never had the funds to spend hours shopping like some girls, she did enjoy just window browsing and being a people watcher.

"We had a norther yesterday, it almost froze last night, and now today, I am ready to shed my jacket in this sunshine. Gotta love Texas weather," Mae commented, leading the way toward the main steps of the courthouse. Just as they reached the bottom, the doors opened and a couple of tall lawmen, their badges denoting them as such, exited the building and stopped as they reached the two women, hats going off their heads almost in unison.

"Ms. Mae, glad to see you. How are you and Vern doing?"

"Well, he's as ornery and cantankerous as ever."

"And you are as sweet and busy as ever, it looks like."

Mae nudged Emma with her elbow and a loud whisper. "Watch out for these two, Emma. They may be Texas Rangers, but they're a couple of smooth talkers, too." They all shared a laugh at her comment. "Emma Cramer, allow me to introduce rangers, Davis McKenna and Russ Holt. Two finer men you'll never meet. This young lady is joining us to look out for Charlie and get some order in my son's life."

The pair looked at Emma and then slowly shook their hands. "You must be one courageous woman attempting that feat... keeping Cole Drayton in line. You pull that off and we just might have to let you join the rangers."

"If I survive, I might just take you up on that." She grinned back at the two men. They were nice and not bad on the eyes either. Mae had to have read her mind.

"Okay, you two can stop flirting with this young lady. I'll be introducing her to each of your wives next Sunday at church."

The hats went back on their heads but the smiles stayed. "Yes ma'am." Davis grinned at Mae. "I'm sure you will. But if you ever need anything, Miss Cramer, you just give us a shout."

"Why would she need to call the rangers? We have our own law right here."

That statement came from another tall lawman who had stepped from the building in time to hear the last few words. Cole Drayton looked every bit the Texas sheriff. A khaki uniform shirt fit his frame just right. Starched jeans molded long legs and dark brown boots shined on his feet. The cream straw Stetson was angled just right on his head. The badge on his chest denoted his position and the gun on his hip backed it up. If she was seeing him for the first time, she could explain why the sight of him put a hitch in her breathing… he was one very good-looking man. With his clothes on. A quick snapshot of how he had looked the previous evening in the bedroom was tossed away as soon as it had come to mind. That was not how an employee should be envisioning her boss.

However, in her opinion, he outshone the two rangers. But then, she was having breathing problems for a second simply because his appearance was unexpected and she had to reinforce herself for whatever battle was to come. She certainly wasn't attracted to him. That would be ludicrous.

"Indeed, you do. And on that note, we should be on our way. Good day, ladies." The two lawmen took their leave and that left the three of them.

Cole fixed his gaze on his mother, not Emma. "Was

there something you needed, Mother?"

Mae was unfazed by the appearance of her son and proceeded to mount the steps and pass him by, bringing Emma along with her. "No, son, I'm just showing Emma around and want to introduce her to some people. You just carry on."

Emma was aware that Cole did not 'just carry on' as his mother suggested. He followed them inside the building and stayed right behind them down the hall and through the doorway marked "Sheriff's Office". Mae was greeted with smiles and hellos by the people behind the long desk. One deputy opened the gate and allowed them to pass through. Then Emma had gazes locked on her and names being given to her by a dozen or so people as Mae ran her through the gauntlet of staff. There were four male deputies in the office, two females... one at a dispatching console and one at a computer terminal. The other people were workers from the various departments in the building... a couple of attorneys and a bailiff. An older woman, with salt and pepper hair swept up on her head in a top bun, stood up from a desk in the corner. She and Mae shared a hug.

"Ronnie White, I want you to meet Emma Cramer. She's going to be working with Cole and Charlie for a while. I'm sure you and she will talk a few times. Just wanted you two ladies to lay eyes on each other. You both have the same tough job duties... keeping my son in line."

"Your son, their *boss,* is right here."

Mae cast a sweet smile in the speaker's direction. "Yes, dear. I know you are. Shouldn't you be catching bad guys or something? Don't let us keep you."

Emma had to purse her bottom lip to maintain control of the sudden urge to grin at the way Mae responded. It was the look on Cole's face that was almost her undoing. *Good for Mae.* She really liked the woman more and more each second she was with her.

"This way, Emma." Mae was moving again. She went up to the closed door, marked "Sheriff" and opened it, not breaking stride. She came to a halt in front of the wide desk. Emma did also.

"Is there something you needed in particular?" Cole crossed to stand behind the desk, exasperation evident in the line of his body. "We're busy this morning."

"And you just go ahead with whatever you were doing. I just wanted to give Emma a comparison between your office *here*… and the disaster we just left." Mae looked at her.

"You see, it can be managed. He isn't totally hopeless."

Emma took in the solid mahogany desk, with neat folders stacked appropriately, very little clutter at all. A computer neat and ready for use. The round table and chairs in the corner in front of the large windows was pristine and shined. The Texas flag and the United States flag flanked the full bookcase behind the large leather chair situated behind his desk. A photo of Charlie sat at an angle next to the nameplate on the desk. Various certificates, plaques, awards were framed and hung on the walls on either side of the doorway. It was an impressive office.

"I see that. I guessed as much."

"And what is that supposed to mean?" Now his eyes were pinned on her.

Did he think he would intimidate her? He could try. But she needed to be on her guard.

"I assumed you would be a very efficient and no-nonsense sheriff and your work habitat would emulate that. Just an observation."

His gaze narrowed on her. "When I decide if that was some offhanded compliment or a backdoor dig of some sort, I'll respond."

"I think Emma is a very direct type of person, Cole. And we'll be on our way now. You go back to whatever you need to do now. Don't worry about anything. I'm getting Emma settled in very nicely."

"I'm sure you are."

If Mae noted the sarcastic edge to her son's reply, she chose to ignore it. On tiptoe, she did plant a quick kiss on his cheek. For a moment, Emma noted a softening in his eyes and it caught at something in her chest. He was a man capable of feeling. *Imagine that.* It changed when he aimed his attention next at her.

"Leave my office alone at home until I'm there to explain the things you can do… and those you don't need to bother with."

"Yes, sir." She felt as if she needed to follow it up with a salute.

Her hand itched to do so. Would serve him right. But she opted against pushing her luck. It was enough to see the look in his eyes… he knew what she was thinking. He dared her. She simply smiled and led Mae from the office. *Another time, sheriff.*

Chapter Five

"IRRITATING, FRUSTRATING, BLASTED... *woman!*" The words zipped through his mind as he punched the speed of his vehicle higher on the speedometer. Ever since his mother had sailed into his office that morning, followed by Emma, that female had intruded where she wasn't wanted or needed. Emma Cramer interfered with his concentration so that was when he got in his SUV and was headed out to take a call that he should have just let his deputies handle. But he needed air. Only it just made matters worse. Now he had time for Emma Cramer to intrude in the silent confines of the vehicle without competition in his brain.

"I don't need help with Charlie. We were doing just fine."

Really? Sure about that? Cole grimaced. Was his conscience going to argue with him now? Okay, so maybe his mother was *partially* right. Charlie was getting older. His mom wasn't getting any younger. She had given over most of her life the last five years to his daughter. *And whose fault was that?*

Jimmy... his brother, that was who. He did this to their

family. He and his devil-may-care attitude, along with his conniving, thieving ways. Cole made certain to include those attributes to his absent brother's repertoire of evil deeds. Add home-wrecker, wife-stealer to the list also. *Can't forget that. Wife-stealer.* The thought brought back a vision of the woman Cole had married six years before... *Pamela.* Bile rose in his stomach and he pushed it down. He hated the feeling in his gut when he allowed that woman and his brother to intrude upon the life he had rebuilt without them in it.

He didn't know what made him the angriest... the fact his own brother had betrayed him in such a way or that his loving wife had been too loving and spread it around... most notably with his own brother. The two of them deserved each other. But what he could never forgive or understand was how any mother could walk away from her baby... just six months old... without a glance back. How could he have been so wrong about someone?

Really? Remember? One look at that killer body in a scanty bikini at the beauty contest you were supposed to judge and then she gave you a smile and you were a goner. Hook, line, and sinker like an old catfish from the pond. A few hot nights on a blanket beside the pond and before he knew it, he was in front of a justice of peace and a married man, with a child on the way. What was the saying? Marry in haste and repent in leisure. Well, he had done that in spades. And he had been taught a valuable lesson. She had duped him. And no woman was going to do that again. *Don't trust your heart or emotions.* That would get him in deep trouble and then rip his guts out in a heartbeat. Brains... common sense. *Keep your guard up.* A woman would use the heart to gain control and then a guy was vulnerable. He didn't plan to ever be that vulnerable fool again. He and Charlie were a team. They would do just fine on their own. Emma Cramer was just a bump in the road. She'd be gone soon enough.

And then what of Charlie? Charlie couldn't be allowed to get too attached. He needed to keep an eye on that. That might mean he had to find a way to spend more time with her. He had been trying to do that. Well, he'd just have to make it top priority. He could guard his heart from any other females plying their trade... and there was more than enough in McKenna Springs and throughout the county he came across. It seemed there were too many unmarried women at times. And there were a few married ones that certainly had no qualms about wanting to help him get past his broken heart.

That was more his brother's style, not his. Once upon a time, Cole had believed a person found the one they were meant to be with, they got married and lived happily-ever-after. Like his mother and father, and his grandparents before them. He had sure screwed up the family winning streak. Something else to not be proud about. His grip tightened on the steering wheel. He'd like to tighten them around his brother's neck. It was a good thing Jimmy and Cole's ex had left town when the scandal broke. It had been tough on Cole, but it was also tough on his parents. They had, in a way, lost a son.

He was aware Jimmy kept in touch on a sporadic basis... usually when he needed a loan. His parents did not speak of him in Cole's presence and that was all he asked. As for Charlie, the time would come when she would have questions. He dreaded that time. The scab would be ripped off the wounds and they would have to relive a past he wanted buried for good.

In the meantime, he would have to keep his guard up around Miss Emma Cramer. Her big, deep blue eyes and curvaceous body would not get past his defenses. He was her employer and she was an employee. And he wished he could keep other thoughts of her out of his brain... if only he could erase certain episodes such as the night they met... in his bed and the way the feel of her body both surprised him and made him ache for things he had not felt in a long time. He blew out an aggravated breath and increased his grip on the steering wheel. Emma Cramer's time was limited in his county and his home. Then he would send her on her way. That was the plan.

THE SQUEALS OF cheerful glee had only abated a couple of

decibels between the school and the farmhouse. They increased again once Charlie set eyes on the puppy that was jumping up and down in its own dance of happiness. Charlie fell to her knees and gathered the furry creature into her arms, wet puppy kisses swiping her cheeks. Giggles and more giggles followed and Emma and Mae joined in.

"I haven't seen her this happy in I can't remember when," Mae said, wiping a bit of moisture from the corner of an eye. "Already you've made a difference."

"I won't take credit for this. Angel is the culprit in this one. I think your son may be right about one thing. It will be next to impossible to separate those two when it comes time for me to leave."

"And we will cross that bridge when it comes." Mae said no more, she just turned and went back inside the house.

"Can I stay out here and play with Angel some more?" Charlie asked the question as if she expected a negative response. "I promise to clean up my room before dinner if I can. Please?"

Emma had to smile. "I saw your room and it passes inspection already. You may play in the fenced yard until I call you to come clean up for dinner."

Mae was gathering her purse and jacket from the counter when Emma reentered the kitchen. "Are you leaving? Can't you stay for dinner?"

"I have a hungry man to feed at home this evening. And it's time I turned over the reins of this house to your capable hands."

"I hope they're capable enough. I've not had too much experience with taking care of a home like this or having a child in the mix, too. I'll probably make a mistake and—"

Mae's hand on her shoulder stopped her flow of words. "Emma, trust in yourself and listen to your heart. You have a good brain and a huge heart. You've just got to trust in your abilities. And I am just a phone call or text away. I'm cheering for you. And I have no qualms about placing my two most precious loved ones in your hands. One step, one day at a time... and you'll make it."

The house felt empty when Mae left her. This was the moment. She was on her own. *Sink or swim. Fight or flight.* That felt more like it. First things first... one step at a time. Good advice. Dinner. She needed to find something she couldn't ruin for dinner. Her skills were basic... and rusty. She only had to cook for herself the last decade or so. Opening the refrigerator, she stopped. *Bless her heart.* Mae had taken pity on her. A casserole dish sat on the middle shelf with a card on the top... *bake at 350 degrees until cheese is melted. Serve with a salad. The mixed fruit cans are in pantry. Charlie loves them with a little scoop of whipped topping on them for special occasions. Your first dinner is such an occasion. Mae.*

Emma shook her head. It was a special day when her path crossed Mae Drayton's. Something inside her had told her as much. Her mother once said that special people came into one's life when they least expected but needed them the most. The trick was to recognize them. Mae was Emma's.

She pulled the salad fixings from the crisper and had a salad made and stored in its container in nothing flat. While in the pantry, her eye had caught on the cornbread mix. She could manage that. She'd put that on when she knew Cole would be almost home.

The thought brought her up short. Cole would be home. *Did he have to come home?* Nice thought but not feasible. He'd be there. She wasn't stupid enough to not know he was going to take some measure of enjoyment in keeping her in her place for the next six months. The man did not want her around... *period.* If it was any other situation, she'd leave. She never stayed where she wasn't wanted. But this was different. She had had very little choice in the situation that placed her there in the first place.

She needed to save up enough money to pay for the repairs on her truck, which was sitting in town, behind the garage, waiting until she could commence with the down payment to get a new transmission ordered. Like it or not, she needed the job. She could put up with almost anything for six months. Besides, she was happy with ninety per cent of the job... good pay, good hours, great living accommodations, wonderful people... all except for one. She needed to remember how bad she had it before and now things were looking better. *Count your blessings, not the thorns.*

The clock chimed five in the hallway. She called for

Charlie to come in and get the scent of dog off her and her clothing. Emma allowed herself to be pulled upstairs by the child who wanted to show off her room to her. Emma had briefly stuck her head in the doorway earlier that day on the tour Mae had given her, but now, she was given the deluxe tour by the owner herself. Emma took a seat on the end of the bed. Purple explosion was the way to best describe the room.

"Let me guess. You sort of like the color purple?" She ventured with a grin at the child.

"I do! It's the best. What's your favorite?"

"Purple."

"Really? It's the same as me?"

"*Really.* I have always loved purple... well, maybe I like a shade of it better now... lavender. But it's in the purple family."

"That's so cool! We're alike. Do you think Angel can come inside to my room?"

Nice how Charlie had snuck that one in there. Emma had to smile. She knew the inevitable question had to be coming sooner or later. "Well, for a dog to come inside, you have to know that it's potty-trained and that takes work. You have to really teach them to be good and have manners. Do you think you have that kind of patience?"

Charlie's head nodded in fast movements. "I promise I can."

"And then you have to have your dad's permission to let

the dog come inside."

The wide grin left the child's face. "He won't do that."

"Maybe if you show him how hard you've worked and what manners you've taught Angel, he might change his mind. You never know until you try."

"I'll work really hard. Will you show me how?"

"I'll show you how, but the work is up to you. Each day, after you get home from school, you need to spend time with Angel... not playing, but teaching. There will be play time later. But you have to maintain a daily schedule for her."

"I'll do it. You'll see. She'll be the best dog ever."

Emma couldn't help but smile at the determined look on the Charlie's face. "You wash your hands and face, and put away your coat and boots, and I'll let you know when dinner is almost ready. You can help set the table."

Surely, Cole would be home by six? Emma eyed the clock over the stove. She would go ahead and mix the batch of cornbread. Once that was done, she ran upstairs to change her clothing. Her wardrobe was meager. She had four office outfits she had saved for and were on hangars ready for an office. A couple of skirts, a pair of slacks, and then the rest were jeans and pullovers and tee shirts. She needed to add to the closet... especially if she were expected to go to church and other outings as part of the Drayton family. An employee... *not* family... but still she wanted to bring them no shame.

A pair of jeans and a turtleneck sweater in emerald green

was good enough for dinner. A pair of brown flats replaced her usual sneakers. She unbraided her hair and brushed it out. It was thick and full and fell past her shoulders. She had toyed with the idea of getting it cut shorter one day. In the meantime, she added a green fabric headband and that was it. Tiny silver studs stayed in her ears most times. They had been a graduation gift from her favorite teacher in high school. She liked to think they brought her luck... or at least added to her confidence. Why were her nerves so jumpy? Everything was under control. All was in its place... dinner, Charlie, her... but not Cole. He was the fly in the ointment. She checked on Charlie who was intent on tying her shoes just right. Then she returned downstairs, checking out the front window for any sign of a vehicle approaching. Nothing. Was he doing this on purpose?

The clock struck the half hour. *Okay. That did it.* Charlie needed to eat because her bedtime was eight. She had to have her bath and get ready for bed before then. It wasn't up to her to call him either and see what time he would honor them with his presence. They would have dinner and he could eat a sandwich. She vented her anger through succinct movements in the kitchen. Charlie came in and Emma took a calming breath or two. No use showing the child what she thought of her father's rudeness.

Charlie carried the two placemats Emma had given her toward the bar. She could barely reach the top of it. Emma stopped her.

"No sweetie. Let's put them on the table in the dining room. I turned the light on in there for you."

"We're eating on the big table? Is it a special day?"

"Special day?"

"Like Christmas or my birthday?"

"I see. You usually eat at the big table on special days only? Well, yes, this is a special day. It's our first meal together. You and I will celebrate."

Charlie was all in with that idea. She put the mats on the table. Emma helped her carry the utensils and place them where they should go. She could tell Mae had been working with her on these skills, too. The plates went next and then the glasses... one with water and lemon for Emma and one with milk for Charlie. Emma stood back and looked at the table. She moved over to the china cabinet in the corner and took out two candlesticks. Lighting the tapers, she set them in the center of the table. Charlie's grin was wide.

"Now, let's check on the food in the oven." Emma put on the oven mitts and brought out the bubbling casserole filled with cheese enchiladas. The salad came out of the refrigerator. The cornbread was next from the oven. She fixed a plate for her and one for Charlie and carried them into the formal dining room. Soon, they were seated at the table. Charlie followed her example and put her napkin across her lap.

"Do you usually say a prayer at dinner?"

Charlie nodded her head and clasped her hands together.

"Then why don't you say it tonight?"

Charlie recited one she must have been taught by Mae... short and sweet. Then she added a postscript. "And thank you for bringing Angel and Emma to live in our house. Amen."

It was simple but it touched Emma that Charlie added her. She was a sweet little girl and Emma was afraid Charlie already had stolen a much bigger place in her heart than she had wanted to surrender.

The food was amazing. Mae would have to give Emma the recipe... if not lessons... on how to make the enchiladas. Charlie informed her they were her favorites. Just like her daddy. *Great.* Well, she would make them for Charlie... not for the man who was still not present. His absence didn't seem to faze Charlie.

"Is you dad usually home late? Does he miss dinner a lot?" She asked the questions casually enough. Charlie was already intent on the fruit cup with the scoop of cream on top.

"Sometimes. He has to work a whole bunch. But granny and gramps usually eat with me. I wish daddy could eat with us, too."

It was said casually enough. But Emma felt renewed anger that the man was throwing away precious time with his little girl. Some people didn't know how lucky they were. She knew the feeling of loss and abandonment at an early age when her own father made it clear that there were other things more important than spending time with her. Like his interest in the nearest pool hall and the inside of a whisky bottle. For Cole Drayton, it appeared his work was the culprit stealing precious time and memories.

"May I please be 'scused?"

Emma hesitated a moment. "Oh, you mean may you be excused from the table?"

Charlie nodded. "'scused... excusid..."

"*Excused.* And yes, you may. Keep working on the word." She smiled at the child. "You'll get it in no time."

The child paused in the doorway. "What about Angel? It's cold and dark outside."

"I'm making her a bed in the mudroom tonight. She'll be warm and just fine. We'll have to see about getting her a bed tomorrow. Maybe we'll go look after I pick you up from school. Would you like that?"

"Oh, yes! And maybe we could get her a sparkly collar too? Purple!"

The shopping expedition was growing in importance. Emma needed to think a bit more on ideas before she tossed them out so freely with the child in earshot. Charlie raced off to her room.

Emma cleared the dishes, filled the dishwasher, put away the leftovers. Then she settled Angel into the mudroom, spreading newspapers and placing a blanket in the corner. Her water dish was in the opposite corner. She didn't need her food dish at night. They needed to establish schedules.

Upstairs, she found Charlie sitting patiently on her bed with her chosen pajamas and house shoes. She let her lead the way into the bathroom where Mae had been right… an array of plastic bath toys had to be placed out of the way before the tub was filled. Then bubble bath had to be chosen.

Emma soaped her blonde locks for the child and helped rinse them. Then she allowed her time to enjoy the water for a bit… keeping an ear open and an eye now and then on the child while she turned down her bed covers and turned on the lamp beside the bed. Once Charlie was all toweled dry and fresh-smelling in her pajamas and fuzzy purple house shoes, Emma sat down on a stool and began to dry her hair with the dryer and brush it out in long strokes.

"You have beautiful golden hair. Just like a princess." Her father had dark brown hair so Emma surmised the hair color had to have come from her mother.

"Thank you. Do you wish you were a princess? I do sometimes. Daddy calls me his princess."

Emma smiled. "I guess it would be nice to be a princess once in a while. But I think it's best to just be yourself."

"I'd like to have pretty dresses with sparkles like Cinderella did in the movie. Do you like pretty dresses like that?"

"I used to when I was a little girl like you. But now, I don't think they'd be very practical for me. Once in a while it might be nice to get dressed up and pretend, but then you have to go back to the real world. You can't be Cinderella all the time."

"I guess so."

"Hop in bed. Does your daddy read you a story before you go to sleep?"

"Granny does."

Emma picked up the book filled with different short stories. She settled the stool closer to the bed. She had Charlie pick the one she wanted and then she began to read. Charlie's eyes began to droop as the long day full of surprises took its toll. Tucking the covers more securely around the child, Emma put the book back on the table and turned out the lamp. Then she hesitated.

Bending down, she placed a soft kiss on Charlie's forehead. "Sweet dreams, princess."

Downstairs, Emma made certain the doors were secured. The lights were on outside. Then she filled a plate with the leftovers from the meal. As much as she might like to dump them and leave Cole with a peanut butter sandwich for his dinner whenever he arrived, she thought better of it. There was another way to get her point across. She set a place setting at the table, made it as nice as it had been for her and Charlie earlier. She left the candle unlit. Hopefully, he would get the message. Then she went upstairs to bed.

Chapter Six

TAKE EVERY ONE of his thirty-five years, multiply it by two, add another ten and he might have how old he felt at the moment he finally parked his car in the driveway. He glanced at the dashboard clock. Was it really that late... or early as the case might be? Just after four in the morning. He eased out of the SUV. Thankfully, the lights had been left on at the back of the house. What had started out as a routine traffic stop had escalated into a foot chase, then a barricaded hostage situation that had not ended well for the robber/kidnapper. By the time the paperwork had been processed and initial interviews logged in, the hours had changed into another morning almost.

Going up the steps, he inserted the key in the lock and turned it. As was his habit, he usually didn't flip on light switches in the mudroom because the light from the kitchen stove gave off enough so he could find his way inside. Only the stove light wasn't working or some such, and then his foot landed in something wet and he jumped sideways only to land on a moving lump that let out a howl and that made him lurch against the cabinet where the ironing board fell off its brackets and clattered to the floor while he tried to grab it and then it ended up knocking down a lantern on the shelf next to it and that clattered and clanged as it hit the floor. The curse words that came flying out of his mouth at the same time were none too soft.

A light flipped on and everything came to a standstill.

"What in the world is all the noise? Your daughter is sound asleep upstairs. At least you could have the common decency to try to be quiet when sneaking into the house at such a ridiculous hour!"

The words were hissed in his direction and heated by the blue fire in the eyes of the woman facing him down. Hands on hips, a long length of shapely leg showing from what looked like some robe-thing she wore over her sleep shorts and tank top, and bare feet. He was faced with one sexy... and *mad*... woman. If his mind had been sharper, if his brain wasn't focusing on some pretty fine female attributes at the moment, and his memory of touching some of that soft skin rushing to the forefront of coherent thought, then he might have been able to defend himself better. As it was, he was tired and out of sorts. Who was *she* to lecture him?

"What did you do to the poor puppy?" She gathered the animal up in her arms, speaking kind things to it while her eyes sparked at Cole.

"I didn't do anything to that mutt. And what's he doing here to begin with? And why did you turn off the blasted light over the stove? How was I supposed to find my way in the dark?" He stomped his way past her into the kitchen. Then he remembered Charlie and the stomping stopped. He removed the hat from his head and hung it on the peg beside the doorway. Shrugging out of his leather jacket, it went on the peg next to the hat. Then he faced Emma.

She was putting the dog back into its area, picking up the items he had knocked down, using paper towels to mop up the water from the overturned water dish, and then shut the door again. Gathering the short robe around her middle, she met his gaze.

It held only a bit less fire. "Look, I don't know what your usual routine is, but your daughter missed you at dinner. She missed you tucking her in and telling her a bedtime story."

"I had an emergency. I told you I would be very late."

Emma's gaze narrowed on him, her arms folding across her chest. "You never told me any such thing. I haven't spoken to you since this morning in your office."

"I left you two texts messages. One telling you that I wouldn't make dinner. The next telling you I wouldn't be in until very late. We did have an emergency and I couldn't stand around chatting on a phone at the time."

He took a breath, his hands on his hips. "And why am I explaining myself to the hired help?"

"In the future, you could *call*. I don't stay hooked to my phone. I was too busy taking care of the feeding, bathing, and putting to sleep of your child to watch my social media."

Looked like they had a standoff. Neither of them was

willing to give in to the other. Cole just knew he needed sleep. "Fine! In the future, I will call you. One time. If it goes to voice mail... that's your problem."

"Fine." She passed him and headed toward the stairs without a backward glance.

Damn woman. He was right... already she was trouble. He followed more slowly, aware of the soft scent of some floral fragrance left in her wake. As he passed the dining room, he caught sight of the table. He paused, his hand reaching to flip the light switch. He gazed at the plate of food. He got the message. She wanted to make him feel even worse. And it had to be his favorite dinner, too. Add insult to injury. So maybe he had been harsher than needed. Things had not gone well the last few hours and he might have taken his frustrations out on her. She didn't ask to be there anymore than he wanted to have her there. But, judging by what she had done so far with Charlie, she at least was trying. And that pointed out his shortcoming. He needed to figure out how to be a better dad and still do his job to the best of his ability. And then her blue eyes wouldn't be aimed in his direction... as much. *Five months and twenty-eight days to go. He might not make it.*

THERE WAS NO sign of the man of the house at breakfast. Charlie was up and dressed and Emma had fed her the oatmeal and banana she had been told by Mae was one of her favorite ways to start the day. Emma had toast and coffee. They had the morning meal seated on the stools at the long island in the kitchen. Emma packed the lunch as Mae had left on the instruction sheet. She made certain Charlie had everything she needed inside her purple and pink backpack. *So far, so good.*

The pickup was the restoration Mae had mentioned Cole had worked on with his grandfather. It was red and black and shiny as a new dime. The interior was spotless and the chrome shone bright on the dashboard. Once Emma got past her initial fear of doing damage to it, she relaxed and found she liked the vintage auto… a lot. Charlie turned on the radio, and an oldies station blasted out with a Buddy Holly tune. To her surprise, Charlie knew most of the words and sang along with the music. Emma found herself joining in on the chorus. She shut the music off only when they pulled into the school parking lot. She wasn't sure how rock-n-roll so early in the morning might be viewed by the teachers.

She walked Charlie inside to her class and was surprised at the warm greeting she received from the teacher and her aide that she had met briefly the day before with Mae. They made her feel welcome and said she could come visit their classroom anytime. If they had curiosity about her or the situation, they made certain it was not in evidence. Charlie gave her a wave and then her attention zoned in on her friends around the book table.

Emma wasn't in any hurry to get back to the house. Hopefully, when she did, Cole would be long gone. She decided to stop and check out a couple of the stores Mae had told her about earlier. She was coming out of the second one when a shadow fell across her pathway. She looked up from digging in her bag to find the car keys and the smile she had placed on her face to greet whoever she might be crossing paths with faded quick enough.

"Surprised to find you shopping so early in the day. Already bored in the country, I suppose?"

"I am equally surprised to see you walking around so early Sheriff Drayton, after your late-night or should I say early morning escapades."

It was clear he made an effort to not speak the first words that came to his mind after her reply. His tone was even and civil when he did speak. "I was on my way to the diner for a cup of coffee and some breakfast. I'd be pleased if you would join me. We haven't had much time to go over your duties without others around."

It was clear he was referring to his mother. *So, this is where he lays down the law.* "I don't suppose a cup of coffee would take too long."

They walked across the street and down the block. He held the door for her and she politely thanked him. Once seated in the booth toward the back of the diner, she felt she could breathe a bit more. Of course, there were more than a few inquisitive glances thrown their way. Many bid good morning to their sheriff and nodded to her. She felt her smile might freeze in place.

"Good morning, sheriff," the woman said, bringing a mug of coffee and setting it in front of the man. Then she looked at Emma and gave her a wide grin. "And you must be the latest talk of the town, the pretty filly that is keeping our sheriff company."

There was a splutter of coffee and a quick grab for the napkin holder beside him. Cole sidestepped having dribbles of the brew down his shirt front. "Darcy, what in the blazes?"

"Thought that would get him. Pays you back for that joke you made about the cherry pie I brought to the council meeting the other night." She turned her attention to Emma. "I'm Darcy McKenna. I own this diner and I grew up with this guy so I can get away with a lot of things. Mostly, I just like keeping him grounded whenever he starts getting too big for that hat he wears."

Emma had to laugh. She immediately liked this woman who was about her own age. "McKenna? I met another McKenna, the—"

"Let me guess, about a foot and a half taller than me… big hat, big gun."

"That's him."

"That's my brother, Davis. He got the brawn and I got the beauty."

"I see that. I'm Emma Cramer and it's very nice to meet you."

"Well, it's nice to meet you, Emma. You come in any time. We can gossip about you-know-who when we don't have anything *better* to talk about."

"*You-know-who* would like to order breakfast, if you have the time to take the order." Cole spoke up at that point, throwing one of his looks at the woman.

"And your breakfast is on its way as we speak," she said, nodding toward the waitress who moved their way. "It started cooking when we saw you walk in the door." She looked at Emma. "What can we get you?"

"Just coffee, please. I ate earlier with Charlie."

"Isn't she a doll? Can't imagine they're related at times." She shot another look at Cole as she headed to retrieve another coffee mug.

"She's great. I like her."

"Why? Because she has an attitude, also?"

"Because she speaks her mind and is friendly and made an effort to make me feel welcome. I can appreciate that."

"Here you go," Darcy said, setting the coffee in front of Emma. "I'll leave you now, but if you need me to come back and see he behaves himself, you just give a yell."

Cole did not respond but kept his attention on his plate. Emma took a few sips of her coffee while he demolished half the pancakes on his plate. She waited for whatever was on his mind.

Taking another sip from his mug, he pushed his plate back a bit and squared his shoulders. His gaze fell on her and for the first time, she realized that his eyes were a shade darker than Mae's... almost a gunmetal color with a darker ring barely perceptible around the irises. Mesmerizing almost. How did she miss them the first time? He was staring back at her. She pulled her thoughts back to where they should be.

"You had something to say?"

He seemed to have to bring his mind back from wherever it had gone also. "Yes... that's correct. I think you know that I wasn't exactly for this idea of my mother's. I'm still not. But part of it does make sense. My mother's in need of some time off. She's put her life to the side and taken on a lot of things to do with Charlie. I'm agreeing to the arrangement she made with you because of her. And if you're as good on the computer as she seems to think you are, then you might be of some help in the ranch office. And I'm sure Charlie will like the company. But it isn't anything long-term. We all need to understand that. This isn't a permanent job."

"You don't need to worry about my not understanding this isn't permanent. I told your mother and I will tell you, I have my plans in the city and they don't include staying very long in this country town. I wouldn't be here now except for the problems with my truck. But make no mistake, sheriff. While I *am* here, you'll get more than an honest day's work from me and the best care I know how to give to Charlie. In return, I expect to be treated with respect. Are we agreed?"

His expression was thoughtful and he didn't respond right away.

Then he extended his hand across the table to her. "We are agreed."

She placed her hand in his and they shook.

Big mistake. Something changed in that moment of contact. It wasn't a lightning bolt or a sonic boom. No bells and whistles. But something had removed the blinders and she saw the man seated across from her. Really saw him for the first time. Was he aware of the same thing? He had a bit of dazed look. Neither of them spoke. The hand contact broke when Darcy returned to the table.

"Hope that was a good deal you were shaking on there. More coffee?'

"No thanks, Darcy. I have to get to the office." He reached for his hat and drew it down on his forehead.

Emma gathered up her purse and bag from beside her. "Me, too. I have to get busy."

Cole stepped aside to allow her to move ahead of him to the register at the end of the bar. While he paid the bill, she glimpsed the newspaper and saw Cole on the front page. "Sheriff Saves the Day" was the headline. She quickly read over the print. Her stomach had a funny feeling. She didn't say anything until they were on the sidewalk headed back to their vehicles. He stopped at hers first.

"I see it got you here safe and sound."

Emma took a moment to register what he meant. Her

mind was still back on the news story she had read. "Yes, it's really a great truck. You can be proud of it. I promise I'll only drive it when necessary and take very good care of it."

Was that a half of a smile? Her breath caught in her throat. It did transform him into something more human. And much more likeable. *Don't get carried away.*

"I know you'll take good care of her and do drive her all you want. She needs to be used more."

"Look, last night or this morning rather… I overreacted. I should have known you were tied up with your work. I just saw the newspaper. What you did, well that was far more important than being on time for dinner. You rescued a kidnapped couple and I acted like a shrew when you got home. You don't need to have that hit you after such a stressful day. I'm sorry."

"Newspapers tend to exaggerate. But it does point out the fact that in my line of work, I can't always be someplace on time… even when I *do* try. And I promise I will do better about that. In fact, I will be home for dinner this evening. No later than five. If you thaw some steaks from the freezer, I'll fire up the grill. We may not have too many nice evenings to grill out before the weather changes permanently on us."

She had to allow her smile to show her partial belief in the time he said. "I'll have everything ready at *six*."

"Sounds fair." There was the upturn of one corner again.

And she needed to not look too often at his mouth. It

could be habit forming... and not something an employee did with her boss.

They were actually behaving as normal adults... *imagine that*. She hated for the moment to end. But it had to do just that.

"And I appreciate your apology and I offer one in return. I guess I could work on the rough edges of my own manners. Have a good day. And tonight, after dinner and all, we can go over a few things in the office that you can start on tomorrow."

"Sounds like a plan." She slid inside the truck and he closed the door before stepping back on the curb. She was conscious of the fact he stood there and watched as she backed out and then headed toward the road to the ranch. She glanced in the mirror and saw him turn towards his vehicle. He definitely was a good-looking man. Why hadn't he been taken out of circulation by one of the single ladies in town? She returned her concentration to the road ahead. There were always surprises when she least expected them. And *he* had certainly surprised her... in more ways than one. She just wasn't sure if that would turn out to be a good thing or not.

Chapter Seven

Charlie had a memory like a steel trap. As soon as Emma picked her up from school, she asked which store they were going to in order to get a bed and collar for Angel. It was a good thing Emma had scoped those things out earlier that morning in town and found the store that would be best for their shopping trip.

As they entered the store, Charlie pointed out another important need. "And since Angel has a collar, she'll need a name tag, too. And she needs a leash for when we go someplace and she needs to be safe when we walk. And she has to get shots so she won't get sick."

"And how did you get to be such an expert on what a responsible dog person needs for their animal?"

"My friends, Julie and Andy. They have dogs and they told me. And we need treats for when she does good in her learning stuff. Like when I train her so she can stay in my room."

"Well, remember what I said… you have to get your dad's permission on that. Maybe you should talk to him about it tonight at dinner."

"What if he isn't there?"

"I have a feeling he will be tonight."

Charlie gave her a look of partial disbelief. Emma simply smiled. *Please be there tonight. If only to make your daughter believe you do want to be.*

"I wish we had found a purple bed." Charlie voiced some disappointment on the return trip home.

"We found a purple leash and collar. And her name tag is purple and white with little sparkles. She'll love all of that." Emma wasn't quite certain Angel was a *bling* sort of girl, but she wouldn't burst Charlie's bubble. "Besides, she doesn't know the difference unless you tell her."

That got Charlie's attention. "How can she not know it's purple?"

"Because dogs are color-blind. They don't see things in color like we do. So, to Angel, it could very well be whatever color you want it to be."

"Wait until I tell Julie at school tomorrow! I bet she doesn't know that."

Crisis averted. Once they arrived home, Emma gave Charlie the task of wiping off the patio furniture outside with the rag she gave her. The Texas winds had brought in a fine coating of dust. And they hadn't been used in a while either. She wrapped the baking potatoes and placed them on a rack in the oven. She found some corn on the cob and brought those out. Perhaps Cole would want to put those on the grill, too.

The phone rang that she had set on the edge of the island as she worked. Was it Cole calling to tell her he couldn't make it? A sudden shaft of disappointment hit her as she reluctantly clicked the call on.

"Hello?"

"It's Cole. Have you started dinner yet?"

She was right. He wasn't coming. "Yes, but I can cancel it."

"No... what made you think you needed to cancel it?"

"I thought you might have to work... that was why you were calling."

"Sorry, but no, I am not working tonight. Although I'm not sure you'll be happy to hear what I did a little while ago."

"Go on." What was she not going to like?

"I bumped into dad and mom at the barbershop. I mentioned grilling and—"

"Did you invite them over? I hope you did. She was so nice to send that casserole over the first night and—"

"If I can get a word in edgewise here, I'll tell you *yes*, they *are* coming tonight. Mom is bringing dessert and said you weren't to worry about that. Are you sure you're okay with the change in plans?"

Was he really worried she might not like it? *How odd.* "I'm really glad they're coming. I enjoy being around them. They were really sweet to me."

"I know." Something changed in his voice. "It's clear I

have some work to do to rate as high as them and Charlie on your list of favored people."

"There's always hope." She tried to play the moment off, but he was not jumping onboard. "Anything else?"

"No. I better get some work done so I can get there and get the grill going." He clicked off.

Why should it matter to him if she liked him or not? They had just decided to be civil to each other. He was a mystery. But she wasn't going to unravel it at that point. *Get moving.* There were more potatoes to wrap and more corn to pull out of the bin. Her phone rang again. It was Mae.

"Are you sure it's okay we come over for dinner?"

"Of course, I'm sure." Besides, she wanted to add… she was only the hired help, not a member of the family or a wife or anything… and that thought shut down her thought process for a moment or two. Where had that come from?

"Hello? Emma, do you hear me?" Mae's voice brought her back to the matter at hand.

"I'm sorry, yes… you were saying?"

"Cole told you I'm bringing dessert? And how about a macaroni salad? He does like that."

"That sounds good."

"And Vernon wants to know if you want him to walk you through the making of the marinade for the steaks? They only have a couple of hours, instead of the usual six, but they'll still be good."

"Okay, yes. That would be great." She listened as Vernon

got on the phone and took her step by step through the process, beginning with finding the ingredients in the large pantry. The steaks were soon covered and marinating on the bottom shelf of the refrigerator.

This would qualify as her first dinner party, as it were. That realization hit Emma as she set out the stoneware they would be using. She had found a red and white checkered tablecloth at the store and she was glad she had bought it. It made the table look more festive. She wanted to make it a little special. The others wouldn't realize why, but she would know. Having a backyard barbecue with family and friends gathered around was one of those daydreams she allowed herself a time or two growing up. Now, it had become reality… in a manner of speaking. The place settings were laid out, with Charlie's help. Then they both went upstairs to get ready for their guests.

She helped Charlie get ready first in a pair of denim overalls and bright purple shirt with ruffles at the cuffs. The child chose a pair of purple shoes to go with her ensemble. Emma found a couple of purple hair ribbons in Charlie's closet and brushed her hair into cute 'dog ears' on either side of her head, secured with the ribbons. Charlie was most pleased with her reflection in the mirror, tossing her head back and forth to watch the dog ears swish around.

"Why don't you wear your hair like this tonight, too?" She turned to face Emma. "I think it would be cute. We could match."

"You do? Well, I think I might just do one ponytail for me. You can be special and have two." *Another coup in child psychology? Who knew she might be good at this?*

Twenty minutes later, Emma was done. She had a sundress that she hadn't worn. She had bought it on a lark one day and it was on sale. Someday, there would be a chance to wear it. Well, the weather was holding steady and the evening would be nice, so why not? It might be the last chance for a while.

It was pale yellow with little blue flowers embroidered here and there on the full skirt. The neckline was square cut with wide straps that left her shoulders and arms bare. She had a pair of gold flats to wear with it. She slicked her hair back into the ponytail as she promised Charlie and found a yellow ribbon which Charlie graciously allowed her to borrow. When she spritzed on some of her lavender body mist, Charlie asked if she could also. Emma indulged her.

They were both in the kitchen when there was the sound of someone coming in the backdoor. Cole appeared in the doorway, and was met by a happy Charlie running to him to be hoisted into his arms for a hug and kiss.

"You're home! Emma said you would come and you did."

"Well, I should come more often if this is the greeting I get from my pretty princess."

"Look at my hair, daddy. Do you like it?" And she swung her head to give him the full effect of her dog tails as she called them. Cole laughed at the display and pronounced them perfect.

"And, smell me. Emma put some of her perfume stuff on me, too." He did as he was told.

"Very nice, indeed. I like that fragrance." His eyes met Emma's over the child's head and he mouthed a soft "thank you" to her. It was clear he appreciated what she had most willingly done for Charlie. He didn't need to thank her, but she was glad he made the effort.

"Hop down and let me change right quick. It won't take me long." He took the stairs two at a time.

Emma checked the potatoes in the oven and they were right on time with the rest of the meal. By the time the steaks were ready, the potatoes would be, too. She finished making the pitcher of iced tea. And she put on a fresh pot of coffee because she noted Vernon was a coffee drinker. What had she forgotten?

Cole came into the kitchen and noted the look on her face. "What's wrong?"

"I hope nothing. I'm trying to think if I forgot anything."

"Relax. This is just a cookout."

"But it's with your family and I want it to be nice."

Cole gave her a silent look. He moved to stand closer than he had ever been to her before. Just inches separated them. She had to look up and then up some more. *Next time wear heels!*

"Everything will be perfect. You've done a good job. Everyone here likes you. Just relax."

"Everyone?" The word came out before she could stop it. She saw the darkening of gray in his eyes.

"Yes, Emma. It seems *everyone* does." Then he turned away and put his attention on the refrigerator. She was both relieved and disappointed. What was wrong with her? Was she coming down with something? She couldn't. *Shake it off.*

Cole bent to lift out the tray with steaks. Emma's gaze was caught by the pull of muscles evident underneath the pale blue shirt he had changed into. He obviously kept in shape for his job. His choice of jeans wasn't bad either. Was it too warm in the room?

"Does it look good or what? Nothing like prime beef."

Emma dropped the onion she had been slicing and the knife along with it. Thankfully, she had the island between her and the man. She needed to get herself composed. Of course, he was talking about the steaks... what did she think he was talking about? *What an idiot.* That was what she got for allowing such things to cross her mind. She needed to get used to the fact that he was a good-looking man and leave it at that. Anything else would only lead to trouble she did not need. She retrieved the knife and went back to the onion.

"You okay?" He was standing in front of the island with the steaks ready to go outside. He looked concerned.

"I'm fine. The onion is just making my eyes water a bit and I dropped the knife. All is okay now."

"I'm firing the grill and then I'll be back for these. How did you know about dad's marinade?" He turned from the door to ask.

"He walked me through it over the phone."

"Well, I hope you wrote it down. He never gives that out to anyone. *I* don't even have it. Guess that makes you special." He shot her a wink and turned to leave, but he stopped again. "Before I forget to mention it, you look very pretty this evening, too." Then he was gone.

No matter what else happened, the evening had just been made for her. Two simple compliments, yet they were as meaningful to her as any bouquets or gifts. She was special to someone. And someone thought she was pretty. Why did she also have the feeling that she was treading in awfully deep water… and she had never been a good swimmer? If she wasn't careful, she could lose her footing and fall in over her head. *Remember… you're leaving. He's just being nice probably to make up for his rudeness. It's just dinner.*

"THAT WAS AN incredible meal, young lady. I'm glad my wife twisted my arm to come over tonight." Vernon accepted the coffee cup from her, and handed her the compliment at the same time.

"Twisted your arm?" Mae spoke up. "He couldn't invite himself fast enough when Cole mentioned the word 'grill'."

"Well, I'm glad you liked it. I really didn't do all that much. I'm just happy I didn't ruin the potatoes. I've never claimed to be a cook." She sat down in her chair again. Charlie was busy playing on her swing set with Angel close by. Cole had pushed back in his chair with a satisfied sigh.

"Growing up, did you not have anyone teach you to cook?" Mae asked it benignly enough. She couldn't know she had touched a raw spot inside Emma. *Truth is always best.*

"My mother never learned from my grandmother. And she didn't really have time to teach me anyway. We moved around quite a bit and she worked a lot. I did pick up some things from watching the cooks in the diners or truck stops she worked in. But nothing like casseroles and nice family meals."

Mae smiled. She wasn't being judgmental or showing anything close to pity. "Then if you're game, I would love to share some of my recipes with you. I could come over and we could do it right here. We might even get Charlie involved."

"I think that would be fun. But I'm going to be busy starting tomorrow on the office. I don't want to take time away from that."

"Don't be silly. You don't need to work seven days a week. You do get time off for good behavior, you know." Cole spoke up. "I think you could manage a cooking class at least one afternoon. If you really want to do that. It's up to you."

"Then I would love to give it a try," Emma said, a broad

smile underlining the words across the table to Mae.

"Well, come on woman. The sun will be up in a few hours and I need my beauty sleep." Vernon rose and clapped his hands. "Where's Grampy's sugar and a hug?"

Charlie came on the run with Angel at her heels. Emma was both surprised and honored when Mae and then Vernon stepped forward and gave her a goodbye hug. "We like to hug those we care about around here," Mae explained as she drew Emma in for a hug. "Thank you for everything, pretty girl. I'll call you about the cooking lesson."

The smile did not fade from Emma's face even as she cleaned up, with the help of Charlie and Cole. She took the placemats from the child. "Thank you, Charlie. Now I think it's time for you to run upstairs and get ready for your bath. I'll be up in a few to help with your hair."

Charlie hesitated. Darting a look over at her dad and then back to Emma. "Should I do it now? Ask the question?"

Emma understood. She nodded her head. She stepped back to what she was doing at the sink, even though her ears were tuned in to the daughter and her father.

Cole leaned his hips back against the cabinet beside her, folded his arms over his chest, and gave Charlie his full attention. "What is this important question you have to ask me? If it's about you dating boys, the answer is *no way*. You must be *at least* twenty-five."

"Oh, yuck, Daddy. I think boys stink too much."

"I'll remind you that you said that in another ten years."

Emma stifled a grin.

"So, what's this about then?"

"I'm teaching Angel some stuff. Good stuff and she's smart and she's trying really hard." She paused for a breath.

"Okay. That's good."

"And when she gets real, real good and learns stuff like not going to the bathroom inside the house, Emma said you might let me keep her in my room with me. Please, daddy, pleeeeeese? I promise I'm working hard and she's going to be a good girl."

Emma cringed a bit inside. She wished she had been left out of the conversation altogether. There was a long silence from the man beside her.

"So, *Emma* said I might allow Angel to stay inside with you?"

The child nodded her head. "It was kinda like that."

"I see. You are teaching the dog manners and housetraining her? Just so she can sleep inside?"

"Yes, Daddy. She'll be good. Can I pleeeeese do that and you'll let her stay inside?"

A deep sigh escaped him. "I shouldn't be surprised this day came. If I asked for a show of hands on this subject, I'm sure I would be outvoted." Emma could feel the look he tossed her way. She kept her eyes on the dirty pan she was scrubbing.

"If… *If*… you are successful in teaching that dog where it needs to go to the restroom, I will consider the question again at that time. But I have to be convinced she is trained."

"Thank you, thank you, thank you!" Charlie fastened her arms around his waist as best she could in a tight hug.

"Now go upstairs and do what Emma told you to do for your bath." Charlie skipped from the room.

"Nice double-teaming there. You might have given me some warning." He picked up a drying cloth and went to work on the pan she just sat in the drain board.

"She asked me and I told her it was all up to you, and she had to do the work. But she had to ask you first before any of it could begin."

"I suppose I should be grateful it was about housetraining a dog this time and *not* about dating."

"Don't worry. Those days are still to come." She threw the teasing words over her shoulder as she headed upstairs.

They had finished the bath routine and Charlie was all tucked in. Emma picked up the story book and then paused. Cole stood in the doorway.

"How about your dad reads a story tonight?" Emma asked the question and Charlie's face lit up when she saw the man move into the room. Emma handed off the book and then left the pair to it. She went back downstairs and ended up in a rocker on the front porch. The night was growing chilly again. She allowed her mind to free itself and she simply just sat and rocked. What would it be like to enjoy every evening in such a way? Family gathered around a dinner table, laughter, the ritual of bedtime, and then a nice porch with a rocker. What else could she want?

"Want some company?" Cole had come outside and his voice was low and soothing.

"It's your porch. But, since you asked so nicely, *yes*, company is nice."

He eased his long frame into the rocker next to hers. Neither said anything for a few minutes. Then a slight giggle escaped from her. To her surprise, one did the same from him. They looked at each other.

"Are you thinking the same thing?" he asked her first.

"Well, I was thinking isn't this weird? It's like we're two old people rocking away here..."

"And it's *okay*." He finished the sentence for her. "I think it's more than okay." They shared an easy laugh.

"Guess I've gotten old. Time was when you couldn't catch me sitting still on a porch. If it was the weekend, I was out and gone to wherever there was a dance floor." Cole shook his head at the memory.

"Guess I was *born* old, then," she replied. "I always loved it when I found a rocker to rock in and daydream."

"I imagined that changed when you got older and the boys started coming around. I'm sure your dad had to sit on the front porch with a shotgun."

Emma was quiet for a moment. She felt Cole's gaze on her. "My dad wasn't around when I was growing up. He didn't think being a dad was his thing. Besides, I was more of a bookworm in high school. I studied and read books and that was about it. Then, when I could get an afterschool job, I spent my time doing that."

"What does your mom do now? Where does she live?"

"She died the day before I graduated from high school."

"I'm sorry, Emma. That had to be very difficult." His gaze had grown somber as he regarded her. "You've been on your own ever since? No other family?"

"None. I worked and saved and went to school. That is the sum total of my life."

"Thanks for sharing that with me. I don't mean it to sound condescending in any way, but I think you can be proud of what you accomplished from such an early age."

Emma stood up and so did he. "It's chilly and you said you'd show me your office?"

"Let me grab my briefcase from the SUV. It's got some mail that came today that you'll need to have for one of the reports."

Emma entered the house and decided to wait inside the office. Opening the doors, she saw that the mess hadn't improved all that much since she'd seen it two days ago. She shook her head and moved closer to the desk. Her eyes moved over the stack of paperwork, and then they stopped. Her name jumped out at her. She reached for the paper. It was a police report… he had run a background check on her. Cole stepped inside the room and stopped when he saw what she held. She looked up at him.

"All the things you asked me on the porch and all the

things I told you... you already knew most of them. Yet, you interrogated me just the same. Trying to see if I would trip up in my answers?"

"Interrogation? I wasn't doing any such thing. As for a background check, I think you can understand that I would check out any stranger who comes into my home and is around my family. Just because my mother liked you wasn't a recommendation that someone in my line of work takes as solid evidence. However, I didn't find anything that proved her wrong. The man who did this check for me, Davis McKenna, you met him. He was thorough and he found nothing but people who had positive things to say about you. I purposely had him do it and not someone from my office. Your information is safe and sound."

She dropped the paper on top of the stack. "Glad I passed. Now show me what I need to do to make sense out of this mess."

Cole set the case down and moved to stand at her side. Instead of talking about the business, he wasn't finished with the subject at hand.

"I'm sorry you've taken offense at what I did. In my place, what would you have done differently?"

She wanted to fault him. She wanted to be angry. She was just hurt and that made her feel vulnerable and she hated that feeling. It seemed she always had to prove she was worthy.

"You made your point. You're protecting those you love.

I get that. It's just knowing that people, strangers were digging into my life and examining me like I wasn't… it's just…"

Two strong fingers lifted her chin and brought her around to meet his gaze. "I hurt your feelings. I'm sorry… *truly* I am. I haven't had a lot of practice in putting myself in other people's shoes. I've been accused of being a bulldozer sometimes. And some might think me heartless. But I *am* sorry, Emma. In just the short time I've been around you, I've seen what others have seen. Maybe I didn't want to see it. But that's my own personal baggage coloring the situation. Forgive me. I can guarantee that this report is being shredded and only the three of us will ever know about it. Davis is a good man. And he likes you. Trust me… that's a tough endorsement to get. You and I got off on the wrong foot… more than once since you came. I hope we can get past that."

She should move away, but his touch was oddly comforting. There was a warmth in his eyes and it was reaching inside her and making her think all sorts of ridiculous things. What would it be like if he kissed her right then? *Kiss the hurt and make it go away.* Was she leaning closer? Or was it him? Should this be a good idea?

His breath was warm on her face. Then he stopped. And the moment was gone.

"And this would be a bad idea. For more reasons than I could name right now. But mostly because you'll be leaving soon and I'm not looking to make any more mistakes in my life with any woman. So, let's just chalk this up to a long day and an emotional moment. And I think we can do office stuff tomorrow. I have some time in the afternoon. I would like to think we could be friends despite, well..."

He was fumbling for words. She should put him out of his misery. "Tomorrow afternoon is best. And one can't have too many friends, or so I'm told. And you're right. I'm not looking for permanent here either. Goodnight."

Chapter Eight

HIS MOTHER HAD been right. Everyone around him was right. People sang the praises of Emma Cramer. None more so than his daughter. Cole should be in a good mood. But he wasn't. The *why* of that condition was Emma Cramer. He had put up a wall where she was concerned. Then he had a weak moment. But he put that wall right back up... even higher. And now he was on one side of it and everyone else was on the other. At least that was how it felt.

After that weak moment in his office, he had told her that friendship was all he had to offer. And she accepted that with her own reminder that she wanted nothing to do with him... nothing permanent at any rate. He had come very close to falling into another trap with another female. Pamela had taught him a tough lesson. Why couldn't he just remember that and move on? Because Emma wasn't Pamela and never could be? How did he know that? Should he run another check on her? *Don't be ridiculous.* The first one had certainly blown up in his face.

She said she understood, but she had been hurt. That

had never been his intention. But he had managed to do it anyway. And from that moment on, she had been a perfect "friend". He said that was all he wanted and that was what he got. She was a model employee. She was pleasant. When he ran late in the evenings, there were no more recriminations or looks sent his way. She made certain there was a plate of food for him in the refrigerator to heat when he did come in. She left a nice note for him of what his daughter's day had been like. And he saw Charlie blooming like a little rosebud under Emma's care. Then why wasn't he pleased?

For the last two weeks, they had set a good pattern. He went to work, she had managed to organize the ranch files and had everything up to date from the bills of sale to the genetic testing records and more, and then she picked up Charlie and took care of her. He came home to find his meal on the table and a happy child. Then Emma went to her room or spent time on the front porch and he put Charlie to bed. Afterwards, he stayed awake half the night trying to figure out why he was so miserable.

And his biggest fear seemed to be coming truer each day. Charlie was definitely becoming Emma's shadow. Last week, he had stopped by the house in the early afternoon and found the two females, dressed in overalls, hair done in like ponytails, and digging in the dirt of the flower beds that had obviously been weeded and were being readied for the bucket of flower bulbs that was sitting between them. He watched from the corner of the house while Emma gave Charlie the step-by-step instructions and patiently helped her dig the holes just deep enough and then drop in each bulb. They then patted down the dirt over the spot and went on to the next one.

Charlie laughed and giggled and looked so carefree. And Emma had been much the same. Her blue eyes were bright and animated even from where he stood and he found more than once over the days since her arrival that he had developed a fondness for that shade of blue.

While he had finished his breakfast two mornings ago, Charlie had moved the step stool to the island and stood on it, next to Emma. Emma had found an apron that was child-sized in town and Charlie had it on and was watching in rapt attention while Emma filled the mixing bowl with flour and then added eggs. She passed the stirring spoon to Charlie and Charlie was intent on her mixing job. The woman had great patience and it had made him even more aware of the fact that maybe his idea of keeping himself and Charlie free of any other person in their lives wasn't such a good thing. It was clear his daughter was blossoming with the arrival of Emma Cramer. And so was the house.

He had noticed small things... a couple of bright throw pillows in the living room. Fresh flowers from the nursery in town brightened up the dining room and the sun porch. There were throw rugs in the hall and a welcome mat on the porch he hadn't remembered seeing around before. He later learned the rugs came from Mae. It was quite clear his parents might be just as upset when Emma left them as Charlie would. And then the thought made him not too happy as it once did either. He needed to keep some kind of a grip on his sanity. They couldn't *all* fall under the woman's spell.

A knock interrupted his thoughts and he looked up to see Emma standing in the doorway of his office. She looked good in the dark slacks and red sweater. And there was *that* problem, too. Especially since he had noted of late how too many of the men at the diner or at church or even in his own office had taken note of that fact also. He felt as if his face was in a permanent scowl because he had used it so much to remind them to keep their distance. But, why should he? Let them crash and burn when they found out she wasn't about to be stuck in their little country town any longer than she needed.

"Are you having a bad day?'

Her question brought him back from dark thoughts. He pushed out of his chair and remembered his manners. "I don't think so. What brings you down here? I thought you and Darcy were having lunch?"

"We are, but we've changed our location. I've spoken to your mother who happened to be in the diner at the same time and she agreed it was a wonderful idea. So, she's going to pick up Charlie and take her home with her. You can pick her up at your mother's when you're done here. I don't think I'll be too late."

"Too late? Where are you going?" He was playing catch up.

"Darcy suggested that we drive into Austin and catch a movie and have dinner there. I haven't been there since I was a child and it sounded like fun. Besides, she needs to pick up those huge pumpkins she ordered for the PTA fall carnival next week. I'm keeping her company. You don't mind, do you? I haven't taken any time away since I've been here."

"I don't mind you taking time. You deserve it. It just caught me by surprise."

"Good. I'll try not to disturb anyone when I come in. You and Charlie have a good evening." She was gone.

The clock seemed to move very slowly the rest of the day. Cole found himself looking at it more than usual. He left the office earlier than normal and found his mother and Charlie engaged in a game of marbles at the kitchen table when he arrived at his mother's house.

"Come watch me, Daddy. I'm beating Granny."

He slid onto the bench next to his daughter. "You are? That's great."

"I'm glad that Emma took some time for herself today. She needs to do that more often. I keep telling her she needs to accept more invitations." Mae made the remark in general.

"Invitations? What invitations?" Cole tried to sound nonchalant in his delving for more information.

"Where have you been? There's been two or three young

men who have asked her out for dinner or a movie. But she's been so busy trying to get that office of yours straightened out that she's not accepted any. Now that it's in good working order, she has time to enjoy herself more. You need to encourage her to do that."

"Me? Why me?"

"Because she sees you as her boss. She has such a work ethic. It would be lovely if she could find a good man around these parts and settle down and stay." Cole was certain his mother had taken leave of her senses. Did she not remember that Emma only promised six months and then she was gone? There were only three and a half months left. The time was flying by faster each day.

"Do you think she would stay here *forever?*" Charlie chimed in on that note. "If she gets married, can I be in the wedding? I could wear a really pretty dress and I know it would be purple because Emma loves purple too... or lavender but that's close enough. And then she could have a little girl and we could be friends and—"

"Charlie, hurry and finish your turn so we can get home." Cole had heard enough of Emma's plans or whatever.

"I thought you might like to stay for dinner here? It's bound to be a bit quiet at your place and no dinner ready for you with Emma not being there."

Cole narrowed his gaze on his mother. He had a feeling he was being played. But exactly *why* was the mystery. What was she up to? "No, thanks. We'll be fine. I brought a pizza home that we can pop into the oven."

"Pizza? Oh, goody! I'm ready." Charlie was pleased and ready to go.

Mae walked them to the door, hugging Charlie and making sure her coat was buttoned. She accepted Cole's kiss on her cheek. "Take care and do give Emma my best. I hope she's having a good time this evening."

They got home and Cole couldn't help the feeling of disappointment when he pulled into the drive and saw no lights on inside the house. Had he hoped Emma might have changed her mind or had arrived home sooner than expected? He supposed she was having too much fun to give them a second thought. Good for her.

Angel met them at the backdoor. She ran out into the yard while they moved inside. She was on the third week of her probation having so far passed her housetraining and had been allowed to have more access to the house. Now her sleeping spot was on the foot of Charlie's bed. Cole had lost that battle before he knew it.

The pizza was good and they finished it off with a bowl of ice cream. It didn't hurt to go crazy once in a while, and not have a balanced meal for dinner. He even put in one of Charlie's favorite movies, *Cinderella*, and they sat on the couch together and watched it.

Charlie fell asleep and Cole's eyes shut for a moment. The next thing he knew, there was a gentle tap on his shoulder and he was looking up into a pair of beautiful blue eyes. Emma was home. That lit a spark inside him. He raised himself up as best he could with a sleeping child across his lap. He maneuvered until he could get her in his arms and then he carried her upstairs. Emma helped get her in her pajamas and they tucked her in bed.

Cole followed her back downstairs. The movie was finishing up with the big dramatic scene where the prince slips the slipper on her foot and all is right with the world and then they live happily ever after in their castle. Cole switched the television off. Emma was straightening the cushions on the couch. She picked up the glasses from the table and started toward the kitchen with them. Cole followed.

"Is that what all little girls grow up wanting? A knight in shining armor to rescue them and carry them away on his white horse to his castle?"

Emma turned and looked at him. "That's a strange question coming from you. Aren't you the no-nonsense lawman with no time for such things? But in answer to your question… I hope they don't grow up wanting that because most will be sorely disappointed if they wait for some man to rescue them. Don't get me wrong. I was one of those little girls. I suppose dreams like that got me through a lot. I could go to the pretend world where someone would come along and I wouldn't be alone any longer and maybe my castle might have a porch to sit on and someone to grow old with.

"Every little girl has their own version of the fairytale in their minds. But little girls need to be taught that it's okay to dream about a lovely fairytale world, but that isn't reality. They need to take care of themselves. If they happen to come across a prince charming while they are doing that, then there's their fairytale beginning... not an ending. Now, aren't you sorry you asked? It's late." She headed in the direction of the stairs. But he stopped her.

"Did you have a nice time tonight? You and Darcy?"

"Yes, we did. She's a lot of fun. And I met some of her friends who live in the city. It was a good time."

"Maybe Austin might be a city you'd consider when you leave here. It isn't all that far for you to have to travel. It's a lot better place than Dallas."

"It's something to think about, I suppose." She turned once more. Then came another question that brought her attention back to him.

"Does living in the city mean so much to you? You seem to love the country so much, I just am a little confused I guess."

Emma gave the question a few long moments of consideration. "I do love the country. But I know that for me to make a good living at what I am trained to do, I have to live in a city with those opportunities. I'll just have to get used to that way of life."

"Did Darcy get those pumpkins?"

"Yes, she did. The pumpkin carving competition can proceed."

Cole had about exhausted his questions. Emma gave him a considering look.

"What's going on? Why all the questions about a fairytale and where I might move and pumpkins? Are you feeling okay?"

"I guess I'm just tired. I haven't been sleeping well."

"Maybe you should get a checkup. You do have a very stressful job. I'd say you should take it easier, but I know I'd be preaching to a brick wall."

"You sound like Mae sometimes."

"I'll take that as a compliment. She's a smart lady."

"Yes, she is. And I should probably listen to her a lot more than I do."

"Now that is one of the wisest things I've heard you say. There might be hope for you after all. Goodnight."

Cole didn't tempt fate with another question. He turned off the lights and headed upstairs to his room. He had just drifted off to sleep when a cry woke him. He was instantly on his feet. A second cry had him at the door and into the hallway. He and Emma almost collided outside Charlie's door. They didn't stop. Emma knelt over the child, softly talking to her.

"Charlie, wake up sweetie. Is it a bad dream?" She laid a palm on her forehead.

The child turned over on her side, arms and hands pushing at the covers over her stomach. "It hurts, my stomach." Emma lightly ran her hand over it.

"Should we call Doctor Morris?" Cole didn't like the feeling of helplessness. It was foreign to him.

"No, you can get a very warm, moist towel for me. Then get me a glass of water, and a wastebasket."

She spoke in calm tones and that helped Cole to calm down also. He was back in a very few minutes with what she asked for. She had him slide in behind Charlie and rest her against his chest. Then she instructed to her to drink the glass of water. The warm towel she wrapped around her stomach area. "Breathe slowly, take a deep breath in through the nose and then blow it out your mouth for me. Pretend you're blowing bubbles."

"Maybe we should call the doctor."

"She has no fever and no tenderness when I touch her stomach so we can probably rule out anything serious as appendicitis. Trust me, I had an attack when I was five. Women who've had one and then experienced childbirth say it's worse. I am going to agree with that." She smiled at Charlie.

"What did you have to eat tonight?"

"Pizza."

"And what else?" Emma prompted.

"Strawberry ice cream. Some cola."

"When did you have cola?" Cole broke in at that bit of news.

"You fell asleep and I was thirsty. I didn't drink a lot of it."

"Is your tummy feeling better?"

Charlie nodded her head. Emma shook out the thermometer and then instructed Charlie to hold it under her armpit until they heard the beeping. Emma removed it then and nodded.

"That verifies there's no fever. The warm towel is easing the stomach. One more glass of water down her and then we'll see."

"See what?" Cole had just finished the question when the pizza and ice cream made a return trip from the child's stomach. Emma wasn't quite quick enough to get Charlie over the wastebasket... a good deal of the mess landed on Cole and the bed. Once it all had come up, Charlie was able to relax.

"Okay. I'm going to get Charlie in the shower and clean her up." She looked at Cole and shook her head. "You need to do the same for yourself. Then we need to get this bed changed."

Thirty minutes later, Charlie was under the clean covers of her bed and fast asleep. Cole's hair was still damp. But he was in clean sweat pants and a tee shirt.

"I need a glass of milk and then my pillow." Emma headed downstairs.

Cole followed. "I'm tired but still keyed up. I hate that feeling of being helpless and I only get it when it involves Charlie. I can handle any other crisis just fine."

"She's your child. She means too much to you. That's

why it's different."

Emma poured a small glass of milk and looked at him.

"No, thanks. I don't think I'll be hungry or thirsty for a while."

She replaced the milk carton and shut the fridge.

"How did you know to do all that? And you stayed so calm."

"I just use basic instincts… is there a fever? Did her abdomen feel hard or hot to the touch? When I heard what she had eaten, it wasn't rocket science from there. The only way she would feel better was to get her to throw up or relax enough to go back to sleep. She went the not so pleasant route."

"Well, I'm glad you were here. I don't know what I would have done. Probably called out half the county for my daughter's upset stomach."

"She's a lucky little girl to have a dad who loves her so much." She took a sip of the milk. Then she sat the glass down on the counter.

Cole reached over and his finger slowly wiped the corner of her mouth. Her breath caught in her throat. His gaze stayed on her mouth. In slow motion, he lowered his head and then the tip of his tongue was doing what his finger began, slowly licking across her bottom lip, then the side, until his mouth covered hers and then his tongue slipped inside and she felt a wild zing of heat flare through her body and she was a goner. It was a sensuous kiss like none other.

A pair of strong hands slid around her waist, and drew her against his heated body. And that took care of her last bit of reserve. His palms then moved under the crop top of her pajamas. Her body was already on fire as he used the island behind her to hold her captive while his lower body pinned her in place, making her very much aware of how turned on he was in the moment.

Her hips nudged forward and he moved his hands higher until his two thumbs reached the underside of her breasts. His tongue dove deeper, dancing and teasing with hers. Her body was on fire and she wanted to be consumed by the incredible sensations that made her toss all other thought to the wind. Her fingertips found the soft hair at the nape of his neck and lost themselves in the thickness.

When his hands slid over the sensitized flesh of the bottoms of her breasts, she wanted to pull him inside her skin. Then his thumbs rubbed across the taut points and fireworks shot off beneath her eyelids and a heated moistness filled her core. Her pelvis thrust against his hardness, needing more of him. But it wasn't meant to be. The radio in the console on the kitchen cabinet was beeping. It didn't stop. It was like a glass of cold water dousing a flame.

He pulled away, swearing whoever was calling was living on borrowed time. While he reached for the handset, he did not move away from her. "This better be—"

Emma could feel the tautness in his body change as he listened to the caller. She tried to get her emotions and body back under control. What had they almost done?

"I can be there faster than he can. Call the life flight team and I'm on my way."

Emma was already ahead of him when he turned to her with an expression that clearly showed he was torn. "It's your job. Go."

"I am closest to—"

"It's okay. Move it."

"I feel like I need to say something, but it wouldn't have anything to do with an apology. We'll talk tomorrow." He dropped a quick, hard kiss on her mouth again and then he headed toward the mudroom, grabbing his jacket and hat. There was a pair of coveralls in the mudroom and he shimmied into them in a second. His feet jammed into boots and he was gone.

Emma slid down onto the floor and allowed the ticking of the clock in the hall to slow her breathing rate. Drawing her knees up against her body, she sat there for several long minutes. Her mind and emotions were all over the place. He said they needed to talk tomorrow. And he didn't seem in the least bit sorry about the kiss. And the last few hours… it just seemed *right*. People who didn't know their situation might take them for a family. And that was dangerous territory. It would be too easy to try and pretend they were anything other than employer/employee. But he had kissed her. And that changed things.

Cole said they needed to talk. What was there to say? She

had no idea. In a million years she couldn't imagine herself ever crossing such a line with someone she was working for. But this was certainly a different situation than anything she had ever found herself in... and Cole was hard to resist. Did he feel the same way? His opinion of her the last few weeks had changed. He had become more accepting, had thanked her more often, had *tried* to meet her halfway. Could there be a chance? Dare she take the chance?

Chapter Nine

THEY DIDN'T TALK the next day. Cole had already agreed earlier in the month to attend a judicial conference in New Mexico with a contingent of fellow officers from their area of the state. That fact had skipped his mind. What they did have was a scant five minutes as he hurriedly packed while she fed and went through the morning ritual with Charlie. When he came downstairs, with his bags, they exchanged looks while Charlie was busy giving him an idea of how she wanted to carve their pumpkin when he returned.

"I've got to go. I must meet the others at the airport but I'm picking up Davis along the way, also. I wish I could change these plans, but I can't."

"It's fine. We're going to be okay. It's not like we don't have plenty of people close by to call if we do need something. Right, Charlie?" Emma glanced over at the child and she nodded her head.

"Okay, then give me a hug and kiss," he said as he bent to his daughter. "I miss you already. You help Emma and be my good girl." He gathered his bag and slid his hat on his head. He moved toward the door. Then he stopped. "Charlie, I forgot my phone and it's on the bed in my room. Can you run get it for me?"

The child hopped down and was off like a shot.

Cole didn't waste any time. The bag went on the floor by the door and he took two steps, the freed hand sliding around Emma's neck and drawing her in for a swift kiss before steps were heard in the hallway above them. "I purposely left my phone upstairs. You and I still need to have that talk about things... about how things seem to have changed and all. And not in a bad way. I'll miss *you*, too." He whispered before resuming his spot at the door as Charlie bounded into the room with his cell. He took it and dropped it in his jacket pocket. "Thanks, princess. I already miss you ladies."

Emma stood for several seconds with the spatula still in hand where she had halted it when he kissed her. What was going on? Something had changed. He acknowledged it with his words and his kiss and the look he gave her as he went out the door. *Was it possible?* The words kept flitting through her mind. She felt there was something she was standing on the edge of but a curtain was obscuring her view of it. Did she want the *possible* behind the curtain? If only the answer came as easily as the question did. Something had changed and she couldn't explain it.

"The pancake's turning black." Charlie's voice brought her back to the reality of the moment. She dumped the charred food in the trash. *Don't count your chickens before they hatch.* Her mother's words of warning came back. More importantly, she reminded herself what generally happened when she dared to get her hopes up about something. They invariably crashed and burned.

Four days. Four days she would wait. Maybe Cole would come back and all would remain the same. He might have a change of heart while gone. *Heart?* Was his heart involved at all? Or had the moment and their simmering attraction finally exploded into a moment that shouldn't have happened at all? So many questions, so few answers. *One day at a time.*

"HOLD STILL, CHARLIE. You're wiggling like a worm. I'll either end up sticking you or me with these pins." Mae took hold of the small shoulders and held them steady… again. Then she bent to the hem of the skirt one more time.

"Do you think anyone else will have such a pretty dress? Do you think it'll win the costume contest? The prize is a party at Pizza Joe's and a hundred tokens to play on the games. I can take all my friends."

"Your costume is beautiful and you need to thank your grandmother for all the material she found so that it would sparkle so pretty for you. Just remember that everyone has a chance to win the costume contest, the same as you. And the object of this carnival is to raise money for the food pantry so everyone will have a good Thanksgiving meal who might not have one." Emma didn't want to bring down Charlie's spirits, but she did need to know that there were other things more important than having the prettiest dress at the carnival.

"I know. That's why sometimes I share my lunch box with Annie Williams. Sometimes she has only an old-looking apple to eat that she hides in her pocket. Her daddy doesn't have a job. She's my friend and Billy Anderson isn't anymore."

Emma and Mae exchanged smiles. "That's very good that you share your lunch with Annie. If you had told me about that, I'd have packed extra. I'll include some other things in there from now on. I'm proud of you for doing that." Emma praised the little girl. "And what about Billy? Why isn't he your friend any longer?"

"He made fun of Annie's shoes. They aren't like the other kids'. She shares them with her little sister. Do you think I could share some of mine with her?"

The two women didn't speak for a moment. They seemed to both be afflicted with something in their eyes. They didn't need to make a big deal out of the fact Charlie was showing such kindness to another classmate without thinking it any kind of sacrifice.

Emma smoothed the folds of the dress. "I think we can make some time to go through your closet and do a little spring cleaning early. That can be a weekend project, okay?"

Charlie's huge smile was her reply. Then it faded a bit. "Do you think daddy will be home in time to carve the pumpkin? It has to look good so someone will bid it."

"Bid it?" Mae inquired, rising from her spot on the floor, gathering her sewing items in her wake.

"Their class pumpkins are going to be auctioned to raise more funds for the pantry. Cole was supposed to help her, but with the weather as it is between here and New Mexico, his flight might not make it until tomorrow evening," Emma explained.

"Well, if we need to get your grampy and his whittling knife after that pumpkin, I bet we can. I'll tell him he needs to come by and help you first thing in the morning. How's that?"

That brightened Charlie's face.

"Now let's get you out of the dress and let me finish the hem. He can bring your dress with him in the morning, too. Now, you both are staying for some stew and cornbread."

Emma smiled. "You won't get any argument from me. How about you, Charlie?"

"Nope. And can I please have some chocolate ice cream, too?"

"Only if you eat all of your dinner first and Emma says it's okay. Now let's get those princess duds off. Why don't you run see what Grampy is watching on television in the den? We'll call you two when dinner is on the table."

Mae busied herself at the stove while Emma set the dining table in the alcove with dishes and utensils.

"I spoke with Ronnie down at the courthouse today. She made the comment that she was certainly happy to see the relaxed change in her boss of late. He seemed to be smiling a lot more and even was taking to managing his schedule so he could spend more time at home with Charlie in the evenings."

Emma kept her attention on placing the napkins on the table next. "Yes, Charlie is certainly happy to spend more time with him."

"He was heard praising the job you were able to do with that new program you installed on his computer. It certainly has helped keep the cattle records updated. I knew I was right about you from the first moment we met."

Emma looked at the woman who was stirring the pot of stew. "How were you right?"

"That you were smart and dependable and a hard worker. And you were just what my son and granddaughter needed… a burst of warm sunshine in that dreary farmhouse and their lives." The woman put the lid back on the pot and turned to Emma with a smile of satisfaction.

"That's a wonderful compliment and I thank you for it. But I think you're giving me too much credit."

"You know by now that I don't say anything I don't mean and that I don't know to be true. And I know that the change in my son is because of *you*. And the fact that Charlie is so happy is due to your love and care… those are things I do know. And I will go a step further and say that I've seen you change also. And I would like to think it's because you've come to care for both of them. Am I right?"

Mae's gaze was intent on Emma and the conversation had turned serious in a heartbeat. Emma had no idea how to sidestep the question. And she had the feeling Mae would recognize anything that wasn't the unvarnished truth.

"I do care. I know it's just my job and all… but it would be almost impossible not to love Charlie."

"And do you love my son?"

Emma was shocked into silence. How was she supposed to answer that one? Because until that very moment, she hadn't put any word to her feelings. *Love?* How did one know?

"I have my answer. And I think you just realized your own feelings. Forgive this old woman for being such a nosy busybody, but I think it's best to be direct and not waste time with nonsense words. And this is just between you and me." Her gaze softened on Emma.

"I can't speak for Cole. But if you've managed to bring him back to the land of living again and broken through that wall around his heart, then I will be eternally grateful. Just know that both Vernon and I think you're part of our family already… for however long or short a time you choose to be with us. And we hope it is a very, very long time." She stood up straighter. "Now let's get the food on the table."

A COUPLE HOURS later, Emma and Charlie headed home. Charlie had had her chocolate ice cream and her eyes were drooping. Since it was a Friday night, Emma had allowed her to stay up past her usual bedtime. They could both sleep in a little in the morning before Grampy arrived and then the clock would start running on getting items packed and ready for the carnival. Somehow, Emma had found herself in charge of the cake walk and had a crash course in rounding up volunteers to bake and to work the booth. But with the good cause in mind, people were willing to help and that made her job easier. And it made her feel part of the community that had seemed to accept her into their fold without question and made her feel welcome in more ways than she could count.

The house was quiet and Angel greeted them in her usual happy dance. She escaped outside while Emma got Charlie ready for bed. When Emma opened the back door again, Angel rushed in and straight up the stairs. Her spot on the foot of the child's bed was her beacon. Emma turned off the lights and checked doors as was her usual routine. Climbing the stairs to her room, it struck her how her life seemed to have become a routine that had woven seamlessly into the house, the town, and the lives of those she cared about. *As if she belonged...* and that thought caused that feeling in the pit of her stomach to return.

She didn't belong. Not truly. Less than three months and her time would officially be up there in McKenna Springs. Her truck repairs had already been paid in full with her last paycheck. Her savings would be in good shape when the spring came and it was time to move down the road. But how would she do that? *Be grateful for what you have, while you have it.*

Her mother had said that after each move they made… leaving one town, one roof… and heading off into the unknown. She had learned the lesson well. When she left, she would have a treasure chest full of memories to carry with her wherever she ended up next. She shouldn't ask for more. She told herself that while she stood in the doorway of Charlie's room and watched the sleeping face of the little girl that had come to own so much of Emma's heart in a short time.

And she thought back over the story Mae had shared with her a couple of days before. Emma had finally gotten up her courage and asked about Charlie's mother, Cole's wife. She had always assumed the woman had died.

Mae had grown quiet and looked at the liquid inside her coffee mug for a few long moments. "It's not something that is discussed, but I've often thought of sharing it with you of late," she had begun. "Charlie's mother didn't die. She *left*. She walked away from her family of her own free will. She wanted… she wanted something else, she said. Charlie was just over six months old."

Emma hadn't known how to respond to the shock of that news, so she had remained quiet.

"It was bad enough that she left her child and husband. But this was doubly hard on the whole family because... because she left with Cole's brother, Jimmy. She left with our other son. That's why you don't hear mention of him or see photos. It would be too hard and raise too many questions... until Charlie gets older and wants to know more. Maybe we'll all have a better grip on what to tell her because maybe we'll all be able to understand it better ourselves."

Emma couldn't find the words so she simply had stood and walked around the table and embraced the older woman in her arms. Mae returned the hug and they had stayed like that for several moments.

In the days following Mae's admission, Emma had realized what was behind a lot of Cole's earlier attitude towards her. He was a man who had been terribly hurt, and was trying to protect not only himself but his child and entire family, from more hurt. And when one opened their heart to someone, there was always the chance it could be broken. He didn't know her. He had checked her out and she couldn't blame him. She wished he had explained about his past then... she wished she hadn't been so resentful of it.

His defense mechanism had been to keep her away... to keep a distance. To remind himself and *her,* that nothing was to be permanent. But he had changed somewhat. And to hear the words Mae had spoken earlier that evening... and the fact she had mentioned the word *love*… that had opened so many doors in Emma's thoughts. Could she have fallen so easily and so fast? She certainly hadn't come to McKenna Springs looking for love. But maybe the saying was true… love is where one least expected to find it. And if Cole was really lowering the walls around his heart? Maybe he *was* changing that attitude… maybe it was *possible?*

Another moment from the past week filtered into her mind, a conversation in the car… a couple of days before Cole had left on his trip. It had come about because of Charlie's sudden and intense interest in Christmas and angels. It had begun benignly enough with her question.

"Do you think we can have a big Christmas tree this year at our house?"

Emma glanced in the rearview mirror at Charlie. They hadn't even made it to Halloween yet. Her unexpected question caught Emma off guard. Emma hadn't given Christmas much thought. She wasn't certain what the child meant. "Don't you have a big tree each year?"

Charlie shook her head. "Nope. Daddy says since we go to Granny and Grampy's house for Christmas, and Santa comes there with the packages, we just need a little tree at our house. But I want to have our own tree, a big one this year. With an angel on the top of the tree just like Granny has on hers. Do you think we could find an angel like that one?"

"We can ask Granny where she got hers." *Emma could see in the child's eyes and hear it in her voice, how important that* angel seemed to be to her whole idea of a Christmas tree. "Why is the angel so special? Why not a Christmas star?"

"Granny told me that Christmas angels are special. Sometimes if you ask them for a wish and believe with all your heart, then your wish will come true. I want to ask the angel for my wish."

"It must be an important wish." Emma tried to prompt the child to share, but it was clear Charlie was going to keep her wish close to her heart.

Emma smiled at the child's simple belief. "You can ask your daddy tonight at dinner about the tree."

Charlie did just that. After being more quiet than normal for her during dinner, Emma gave her a little nudge. "Charlie made an interesting request today when I picked her up at school. Would you like to share it with your dad?"

"It would be really, really good if we can have a tree like Granny has at her house. Not a little tree but a big one. I could help decorate it and we can ask Granny where we can get the angel for the top of it. And it would really be fun to have our own tree like that. Pleeeeese, Daddy? Can we have a big tree this time?"

Cole studied his daughter's pleading face. It was hard to read what his thoughts were, and Emma had a swift moment of doubt… surely, he couldn't have an issue with the tree request? Then Cole's gaze fell on her. "And how do you feel about Charlie's request? Are you a big tree lover at Christmas time?"

"To be honest, all we ever had when I was growing up was this little three-foot tall silver tinsel tree. I always thought it *would be nice to have a real tree, though."*

"See, Daddy? Emma needs a real tree, too... a big one... with an angel."

Cole's eyes warmed as they regarded Emma for a moment or two longer, then they fell on his daughter. A smile creased the handsome face. "Then I suppose we should have a big, fresh tree this Christmas."

Charlie jumped off her chair and ran around the table, her arms going around her daddy's neck. "Thank you, thank you, oh, thank you! It's going to be the best tree ever. I can't wait. When can we get it?"

He laughed, scooping her up in his lap. "When it's time, maybe we can go pick one out from Wellman's lot. They always have the best available. But let's get through the other holidays first. Okay?"

"Can I call Granny? I want to ask her about the angel. And tell her about our tree."

"Go for it, princess." He dropped a kiss on her cheek and the child was off in a flash to the phone in the living room.

"You made her very happy." Emma stood and began clearing the table.

Cole did the same. He followed her into the kitchen and began stacking dishes on the cabinet, while she readied the dishwasher.

"Well, it's time to have a proper tree in this house. And I'm glad it'll make you happy, too. I think this Christmas might be one of the best. It's time we put life back where it belongs."

She remembered her mother once saying when she was small and they had gazed upon their small little tree with its meager one gift underneath it. *All sorts of miracles can happen at Christmas, Emma. You just keep believing... one day they will... you'll see.* She hadn't thought about those words in a while. Somewhere along the way, she had stopped believing. Maybe this Christmas would bring a possibility of a miracle with it. Maybe it was time to *believe* again. *Maybe.*

THERE WAS A slight smell of bacon drifting past her nose. Coffee, too? Was she dreaming? Emma turned over in her bed and her eyelids opened a bit. It was early. The clock read seven. There was the burning smell again. Her eyes flew wide and the covers were tossed off her and the bed in nothing flat. Something was burning in the house! She flew down the stairs. She wasn't in the kitchen so what in the world... she needed to call the fire department... get Charlie... and then she came to a screeching halt between the kitchen and the living room. She was framed in the doorway. Her eyes blinked a time or two as she tried to get her heart rate to a semi-normal pace. Two pair of male eyes blinked back at her. *Cole and Grampy.*

"I smelled something... I thought there was a fire or something in here and..." She noted the way Cole's eyes were moving down her body and the upturn of his mouth as if something was amusing. Grampy coughed a time or two and studied his coffee mug. Then it dawned on her. She scrambled back up the stairs and did not stop until she was in her room with the door shut.

She had run down the stairs with just her short nightgown on and nothing else. When would she learn? She needed to invest in some long, granny-style pajamas that covered from neck to toe. Her face burned with embarrassment… mostly because of Grampy. Cole was used to seeing her in such a state… on occasion. What must Vernon think? And he'll tell Mae. *Oh, dear.*

She didn't return to the kitchen until she was fully dressed. That meant jeans, long-sleeved cowl-neck navy blue sweater and her hair and makeup presentable. She wore a pair of soft boots she had invested in the previous week. Charlie had joined Grampy at one of the bar stools and they all smiled when she walked in. Going to the coffee pot, she took her time pouring a cup for herself. Taking a sip, she then put a smile on her face and turned to face the three.

"Good morning. Sorry about earlier. I smelled something burning and assumed the worst. I had no idea anyone would be in the kitchen cooking. Guess it's a good thing I didn't call the fire department before racing downstairs. And I don't usually come down before I'm dressed properly." *Enough. Too much.*

Cole stepped over and placed a plate with a short stack of pancakes and crisp bacon on it in front of her. Very crispy bacon by the looks of it. He had a sheepish grin on his face.

"That would have been my first batch of bacon you smelled. It didn't turn out so well. This batch is still a might crisp, but there's no more so you'll just have to try to pretend to eat it. Guess my surprise really was one."

"I think it's great. I haven't had so much excitement in a kitchen in a long time. I think I might need to come by for coffee on the weekends more often." Vernon grinned at them, a slight wink added for good measure.

"Isn't it awesome, Emma? Daddy made it home in time to help with the pumpkin. Grampy and daddy and me... we're going to have the best one ever." Charlie was so happy at the turn of events.

Emma had to smile. "Well, that is awesome indeed." She finished the last bite of pancake and did manage to do justice to at least one strip of the crispy bacon. "I'm going to have to get a move on. I said I'd be at the school to help set up and then get back here, change and be back to take in the cakes as they drop them off." She looked at Cole then and he had that same strange smile on his face. He must have had a good trip. "If you'll just pop things in the dishwasher, I'll do the rest when I get back." She stood and placed her dishes on the cabinet next to the sink. She slid her purse over her shoulder.

"Don't worry about things here. We've got it covered."

"Mae's already on the road herself this morning with her errands." Vernon spoke up. "That reminds me, she gave me something to bring over and I left it in the backseat of the truck. I'll go get it."

Before he could rise, Cole stopped him. "You sit and make sure Charlie finishes her milk before we think about that pumpkin. I'll go get it."

Emma went out the door ahead of him and she was aware he was right behind her. They reached her truck first. Cole was quick and opened the door for her. She stepped into the space and placed her bag on the passenger seat. Why did she feel like an awkward school girl alone with her first boyfriend? That was the closest analogy she could come up with in the moment.

"Thank you and thanks for breakfast. I can't believe you made it home in time. I thought your flight couldn't get out until late this afternoon?"

He grinned and she marveled at the transformation. He was good-looking before but this new version of Cole Drayton was downright awesome. His smile went straight to her heart.

"It couldn't, but *I* could. I rented a truck and we drove on through."

"But the storm and all…"

"No storm was going to keep me from such an important night for Charlie. And there's some unfinished business you and I need to discuss that's pretty important. I've thought about that a lot while I was gone."

"Me, too."

"I would hope for at least a smile when you said that, so

now I'm worried that your thoughts might not be in line with mine." He had stopped smiling, too.

"I had a talk with Mae earlier this week. She told me about everything... Charlie's mom... your brother... everything. It explained a lot about your attitude when I first came. At least, it did to me. I'm sorry about the way I behaved when I found out about the background check, and however else I might have come across. I know you're protecting your daughter and family... and *you*, from anyone or anything else that might bring another heartbreak."

"That was a bad time. It was a conversation I thought you and I needed to have this weekend. But I'm glad Mom was able to talk about it."

"She lost a son in all of it. There's just so much hurt to go around. But you must know I would never do anything to hurt them or Charlie. They mean too much to me."

"And should I ask if I figure into that equation?" His silver-gray eyes locked on hers and she felt that drowning sensation.

The realization came that she had already gone under for the third time. She was a goner in just three months. *You were right, Mae.* She had fallen in that foreign malady called love... and with a Texas lawman. Worst of all, she had no idea what to do about it.

"If you must take that long in thinking of an answer, I think we should forget that—"

"No!" The word came out a bit louder than she planned.

"Don't get the wrong idea. You *do* figure into it. I... I just think we have things to talk about and maybe this isn't exactly the perfect place." She smiled and waved at the little girl watching from the window.

Cole understood and nodded. "You're right. We'll postpone this conversation for another time when we are truly *alone*." She slid into the driver's side and he shut the door, leaning in through the open window.

A swift kiss went on her check and she felt the warmth rise like a tide through her body. His gaze locked on hers.

"Be careful and hurry home." He stepped back and waited for her to back out and head down the drive. She glanced in her mirror and he was still watching as she drove away. That brought a wide smile to her whole being. *It's possible. It's really possible.*

Chapter Ten

The silly phrase kept repeating itself in her brain all through the day. *It's possible.* She was being ridiculous. She needed to concentrate on other things. But it was hard to do whenever she looked up, it seemed Cole was always someplace in her viewing area. Of course, the courtyard and gym and cafeteria were all pretty much in the same area so it would be hard to not see the same people two or three times… *or more.* And the fact that he was taller than most, and he was looking very *hot*… in the *good* sense of the word… in the deep blue western cut shirt and black jeans, black boots, and black Stetson… *yep.* He was hard to overlook.

"Isn't it childish how some females just make a ridiculous spectacle of themselves whenever a single, good-looking man comes in the room?" Darcy's words brought Emma out of her thoughts and she straightened from the counter and looked at the woman lining up the next selection of cakes and pies to go on the auction block. Darcy had brought a few of the baked goods from her diner and she had volunteered to help Emma, also. They were having a good time of it, too.

"What are you talking about now?"

"Some of the females in this town, who become simpering idiots over some guys when the rest of the time they're usually smart women. I don't understand it. And when the guy is clearly not interested and has already set his sights on some other female, they just don't give it a rest. Pathetic. Shoot me if I ever exhibit any of those symptoms."

"Can you be more specific, or dare I ask?"

Darcy nodded toward three women standing across the room at the dart throw. Emma looked that way and then her attention was caught and held.

"Jennifer, Chloe, and Ashley. They are making fools of themselves over our sheriff there."

Cole was standing with an older couple and the three women were smiling too brightly and fluffing their hair and acting foolish a few feet from him. Emma could certainly agree with Darcy. Her gaze stayed on Cole. To his credit, he wasn't being taken in by their acts.

"They just don't stand a chance, you said? Why do you think that?" Emma dared to ask the question but she wasn't sure she wanted to hear the answer.

She felt confusion. Was Cole interested in someone? Did Darcy know who it was? Did *Emma* want to know?

"Because the man clearly is taken. And we both know by who… or is it whom?"

Emma's gaze swung to Darcy. "*We* know who?"

Darcy looked at her and then a grin spread on her face. "Are you serious? You *really* don't know, do you? The guy is taken. I never thought I would say that. But I agree with his selection, so I'll say it. It's *you*. Cole Drayton has eyes only for *you*. Case in point... he's looking this way right now. And it isn't one of these fine cakes that he's eyeing."

Emma swung her head around and met the silver-gray eyes locked on her. Was she blushing? There was a warmth creeping up her neck and her cheeks were feeling a bit heated. Why couldn't she play it off and be more sophisticated about it? She picked up a roll of tickets and began re-rolling them. She needed something to do.

"I think you're mistaken."

"So, you don't like him. I can let those ladies know they might—"

"I didn't say that, did I?" Then she saw Darcy's smile and knew she had been caught easily enough. "It isn't amusing, Darcy."

"I know. It's sweet. And I think it's perfect."

"You do? What makes you say that?"

"Because I've known him practically all our lives. He's a good, decent man and they are rare these days. And I know what he went through with Charlie's mom and all. He deserves someone good this time. I think you deserve *each other*. And that is all I will say on the subject. Except... if you ever need someone to listen about anything... or anyone... you know where I live. Now, let's sell some cakes."

Ten minutes later, Davis McKenna came by the booth with a pretty lady he introduced as his wife, Stacy. "Just warning you ladies, I intend to win that last lemon meringue pie over there. I've had my eye on it ever since Darcy took it out of the box."

"Then you better buy your tickets and take your chances," Darcy said, holding out her hand for her brother to drop some cash into it. He did just that.

"Do you think you really need that pie?" His wife gave him one of those looks that have specific meanings between married couples.

Emma smiled at how different the tall ranger seemed around his wife. And it was obvious to see that he was quite taken with her.

"I may not *need* it, but I want it."

"Emma, you may not know it, but my brother married *up*. Stacy is a best-selling author. She writes great romances. You'll have to try one."

"That's amazing," Emma said. "I'd love to read one."

"And I should have worn my t-shirt." Davis added.

Darcy rolled her eyes and Stacy looked to the ceiling. "Here it comes."

Emma was mystified. Then Davis clued her in. "I have a shirt that says on the front… 'I married a romance writer.' On the back, it says… 'yes, I am the inspiration for paragraph two of chapter four, page eight'."

Emma burst out laughing. The others joined in.

"He must have told the one about his t-shirt." Cole had walked up to join the group, standing closest to Emma at the counter.

"So, this is a legendary story in these parts?" Emma grinned at the ranger.

"That's one way to put it," Stacy replied. "While you work on getting that pie, I'm going over to the quilt exhibition. I have my eye on that yellow, rose petal one."

Davis watched her leave.

"Yellow rose petal," Darcy muttered more to herself than anyone else. Then her eyes darted to Davis. He pretended an interest in one of the cakes on display. "I saw that one. It's a baby quilt. What haven't you told me? Your favorite sister?"

"You're my only sister."

"Stop being my knucklehead brother and tell me... am I going to be an aunt?"

He didn't get the words out because she saw the broad grin and she launched herself across the counter and was choking him in a tight hug.

"Hey, don't make a fuss. Stacy wants to tell people after church tomorrow."

Darcy gathered herself together but couldn't keep from beaming. "My lips are sealed."

"Mine, too. Congratulations to both of you." Emma smiled at the man.

Cole extended his hand and slapped on Davis's shoulder. "Congratulations, Davis. Having a child... it'll make you a better man."

"Thanks, everyone. We can't wait for this next chapter of our lives. And, now, I think I should win that lemon pie by default."

Darcy shook her head. "No charity here brother. Especially since I practically had to drag that news out of you. So, if you want that pie, you have to fight for it."

"Lemon pie?" Cole spoke up. "Would that be one of *your* lemon pies, Darcy?"

"That it would."

Cole dug in his pocket and laid a handful of bills on the counter. "Give me as many tries as that will buy me."

Emma handed over the tickets.

"You think you're going to get that pie?" Davis eyed the man beside him.

"I know it." Cole smiled back.

"This will be fun." Darcy called everyone to take their places. Emma began the music. They had combined two games… the cake walk and musical chairs. The person who was the last chair left, got to pick their favorite cake or pie. There were eight items left on the shelf… and only one lemon meringue pie.

Twice the guys both lost out early. Two more times and the same thing. They both added more money for tickets. On the sixth go around, it came down to four people, including them. Then the next round… they stayed in. As luck would have it, they were the last two remaining. Two determined men and one chair. The crowd had gotten into the spirit of things. Cheering and booing appropriately.

The music started and Emma closed her eyes. She didn't want a certain person to get any unfair advantage from her... although she was secretly rooting for a certain sheriff. Another few seconds and then she hit the stop button and opened her eyes. Two grown men, one small chair and each were trying to plant their ownership on it. The scuffle was on, the crowd was clapping. And then the ranger timed it just right and knocked the chair out from under Cole who was just about to take the seat and planted himself there instead. Cole landed with a thud on the hard floor. Laughter ensued. Davis stood up and gave a helping hand to Cole. They shook like good competitors. Darcy handed over the much-fought-over lemon pie.

"What say we grab a couple of forks and go find an empty picnic table?" Davis looked at Cole.

"First smart thing you've said in a while. You're on."

Emma and Darcy shook their heads at the pair carrying their pie and being so pleased with themselves.

"Yet another example," Darcy said.

"Example?"

"The difference in Cole Drayton. All the other carnivals? He was in uniform, walking around watching from the edges, providing security. He didn't engage in any of the games. Mae and Vernon enjoyed most of the carnival with Charlie. This year, he's enjoying himself and being a dad. Thank you, Emma Cramer."

"Thank you, Emma Cramer." The words were repeated an hour later by Cole, himself.

They were standing with Mae and Vernon watching Charlie parade across the stage in her sparkly princess costume, replete with tiara and satin slippers. The smile on the child's face couldn't be any brighter as she made a wave in their direction. He leaned toward her and whispered, "That costume idea and working with mom on it in the midst of everything else you already do for us, it means a lot and made a difference to Charlie."

Emma's heart filled with happiness under Cole's praise and thanks. It had all been a labor of love for the child… and her family. And that included the man beside her most of all. It was funny how love could suddenly upend one's world and cause colors and smells and sounds to be bolder, brighter, better. Emma walked around the carnival with Cole and his family and, for the first time, she felt alive and that she had a definite meaning… a purpose and place in life. She was content to bask in the wonders around her.

"You're awfully quiet. Are you feeling okay?" Mae asked the questions while they waited for Charlie to finish her pony ride. Cole had promised her that to help console her from the fact she didn't win the best costume award and the pizza party. A boy in her class came dressed as a "Star Wars" Stormtrooper and that was a crowd pleaser. She did win in the most beautiful category and received a coupon for a free manicure and a small bouquet of flowers, which she had given to Emma to take care of.

"I'm fine. I think the whole week finally winding down is just dawning on me. It's nice to just enjoy things at a leisurely pace now and then."

"Well, you have done marvels in the short time you've been with us. I thank the angel every evening in my prayers who guided you to our family. Truth be told, I can't remember what it was like before you were with us. I think that says a lot. And I hope we've grown in your heart, as well. Just know how much happiness there would be if you decided to stay on in the spring. Now let me go hurry those three up."

Emma was glad she had a moment to compose herself. That was the second time that day that someone had told her what her heart had only admitted and dared to hope could be possible. Still she didn't want to jinx it. It was all too new and too fragile. And Cole was the one that mattered and he had said nothing... only that they needed to have a private conversation soon. *Keep hoping.*

Mae and Charlie left the group for a few minutes to stop at the face painting booth. Charlie wanted a butterfly on her cheek. Cole and Emma, along with Vernon, found a stand with homemade ice cream and sat down to enjoy some cones.

"I need to pick your brains," Vernon spoke, looking around to make certain they were not in sight of Mae and

Charlie. "You know we have this anniversary thing coming up in a couple of weeks and all."

"Anniversary?" Emma asked. "This is the first I've heard of it." She cast a look at Cole, who only shrugged.

"It's our fiftieth. And it's a big deal I know. We got married when we were both just eighteen and I was going off to the military. It wasn't anything fancy. But Mae's never been one to want to have any type of celebration, but I figure this time, we best do something while we're still able to walk and have almost all our own teeth still."

Emma grinned at the man. He was adorable.

"I don't know what to do."

Emma looked at Cole, who looked back at her. "What's going on in that head of yours?"

"Generally, I've heard that the child of the couple is the one who hosts such an important anniversary. So, I think you better get it in gear."

"*Me*? What do I know about throwing something like this?"

"Guess it's a good thing you have me around then." She smiled sweetly back at him.

He returned the smile with a grin. "I guess it is." He looked at his dad. "Leave everything to us. This will be a night to remember."

Emma felt a quick shiver run up her spine. It wasn't from the ice cream. She had a strange feeling and it happened when Cole had spoken those words.

Chapter Eleven

The day after the carnival, Charlie had come down with a fever and then it moved into a respiratory infection, and then strep throat had taken her down. Between doctor's visits and the planning of the anniversary party and things being busy at the sheriff's office, they had been two ships passing in the night.

"Best laid plans," Cole spoke the words as he carried the last bag of groceries into the kitchen and set them on the cabinet. Emma began putting them away. He went back and opened the door for Angel to come in from the backyard. "I need to work on a doggie door for her when the weather gets warmer in the spring."

Emma took note of his words, but he didn't. He was busy going through the stack of mail. His comment might mean he thought she and Angel would still be there then or just maybe it slipped his mind. Emma pushed it away. There were other things to get through first.

"The doctor said Charlie can go back to school tomorrow. Of course, it's Friday, so I suppose that's good, too. She's still a little weak kitten at times."

Cole shook his head. "Strep throat is not something I hope to go through again with her. She was in such pain."

"A couple of the children from her school ended up in the hospital with theirs. We can be thankful she didn't have to do that." Emma finished the last of the groceries.

She kept a couple of the cans of peaches on the cabinet. She took down a bowl and emptied them inside. Then she set them in the refrigerator. "She loves her peaches and they make her feel better. If you'll remember to give her those when you see she finishes her soup tonight?"

"Got it. Will you be late?"

"Darcy and I have the lists to go over and then the menu and the timeline. But I shouldn't be too late. I'll get on the road so I can be back sooner." She shrugged into her jacket.

The night was cold and there was a threat of snow flurries. The season had changed quickly on them. Cole came up behind her and his hands went on her shoulders. He turned her around to face him. It was the first "alone" time they had had in a few days.

"Thank you for being a steady rock through these past few days."

"Not so steady if you could see my insides. Just because I'm calm on the outside, doesn't mean I'm not a wreck at times on the inside."

"The fact you care so much for Charlie means more than I can say. And you're working so hard on this party for Mom and Dad. You don't have to do all these things yet you are. I just want you to know I can't tell you how much it means because words just don't seem to be enough."

The words stopped and actions took over. His hands slid down her back and drew her into the circle of his arms. His lips took possession of hers and she had only time to slide her arms around his waist to help steady herself as her knees felt ready to buckle. Words were nice, but the actions were definitely her preference. The man could kiss and where he led, she willingly followed. Her heart was hammering in her ears. His lips moved over hers, demanding and drawing fires igniting within her.

"I know I said we needed to talk," he whispered against her cheek, "but talking is highly overrated at times." His lips found the soft spot behind her ear and a shiver ran through her.

"I agree." She breathed against his throat as he placed soft kisses across her forehead and then downward until he captured her mouth again.

His kisses were drugs on her senses. She wanted more.

"Once this party is done, we need to take some time... a day or two away from here. Maybe while Charlie stays with Mom and Dad during part of the school holidays. That sound okay with you?"

"I think that's a plan... a good one." Her reply was smothered in another earth-shaking kiss.

If she had *her* wish, they would leave at that moment. Her heart was doing happy somersaults. He wanted to be with her… just the two of them. Maybe he'd ask her to stay… *maybe*. She needed to have her reply ready.

"You need to get on the road. You're late. Just tell Darcy it was my fault." He grinned as he stepped back and she moved to the back door.

She threw him a smile from the doorway.

"If I do that, she'll know exactly *what* kept me."

His laugh followed her outside. And the smile stayed on her face all the way into town.

"This is crazy," Mae said for the third time. Seated in the back seat of the '56 Chevy with Cole driving and Emma in the passenger seat, Mae turned to her husband. "I can't believe you rented this old car to take us out on a date. And we even dressed up for the occasion. What will people think when we go into the diner dressed like this?"

"I rather like these clothes. And they are 'in' right now. I'm told people buy them in the cities. So, everything makes a circle." Emma had fun raiding the attic in Mae's house where she kept a whole treasure trove of clothing from the forties and fifties from former family members. Most of it was in perfect condition. Mae was wearing a black satin, full-skirted dress with hot-pink satin trim on the wide collar and showing on the underskirt of the outfit. Pink petticoats poofed out when she had seated herself in the car.

"Well, you were made to wear these dresses, Emma. That color suits you. Don't you think so, Cole?"

Emma loved the dress from the moment she saw it. It had very full chiffon skirts, a portrait collar, and then huge, puffy chiffon sleeves with wide cuffs at the wrists. It was pale lavender and her three petticoats were white and trimmed in delicate lace edging. Her hair had been styled into a fashionable upswept style that made her neck look long and swanlike, Mae had declared. Much like Audrey Hepburn. Emma doubted that but she would take the compliment.

Cole's gaze fell on her. "I'd say that Dad and I have the two most beautiful dates in the county tonight. Right, Dad?"

"Well, I think that every day, son."

"Oh, Vernon." There was a blush in Mae's tones.

Emma smiled. That was the way marriage should be. She trained her attention out the window as they entered the outskirts of the town. *Darn moisture.* She didn't want to ruin her makeup.

"I've been meaning to ask since I got here," Emma said, changing to a lighter subject. "What brought about this fixation you all seem to have with the fifties? I mean, don't get me wrong, I love the old music and the clothing is great."

"Stuck in a combine for twelve hours a day, six days a week, and having that music as all my dad would allow to be played on the radio, you get used to it and I just liked it after a while," Vernon volunteered.

"And dating Vernon, and being around his parents and

home, I guess I was drawn in to it. Besides, the music in our day and time just never appealed to me. And I do love the styles. It's fun and makes us happy. That's about the best answer I have for it," Mae added.

"I didn't have much choice as you can figure." Cole piped up. "Between parents and grandparents, it just kinda became like a hobby I guess. And I think I've noticed you, a time or two, change the channel on the kitchen radio to catch the oldies station." He grinned at Emma.

"Guilty. I admit it. Although I still love my country music and George Strait, I do enjoy some good fifties tunes... thanks to you all."

"Cole, you missed the turn to the diner."

None of the three people made any reply to Mae's comment.

"Did you—"

"I forgot my wallet at the beauty shop yesterday and Mary has it at the bowling alley with her. I told her I'd drop by on the way to dinner. And she would love to see your outfit. I told her we might all come in and show her."

Cole shot a look at Emma, and a wink. He approved of her swift thinking. So far, they had managed to keep Mae in the dark about their true plans for the evening.

In a couple of minutes, they pulled up to the front doors of the bowling alley that had been in business in the town for over sixty years. Emma realized it was a perfect cover for their plan. Bowling dates were popular in the fifties. They had a large party area where the old roller rink had been and was now open for special events. And Mae wouldn't suspect anything when she saw a lot of cars in the parking lot. In Emma's mind, it had been a stroke of genius.

"Come on, let's all go in and show her the outfits." Cole opened her door and gave her his hand, while she maneuvered her very full skirts without any snags.

Vernon was helping Mae from the back. They were both laughing by the time they managed to exit as gracefully as possible from the car. Cole tucked Emma's hand around his arm and led the way.

It was dark inside the cavernous building, just faint glows from the lane screens kept it from being totally black. The foursome stopped inside the doorway.

"Whatever is—" Mae began but stopped when the overhead lights popped on and several dozen people were yelling and clapping, emerging from their hiding places. *Congratulations… Happy anniversary… Way to go, Vernon and Mae… The best is yet to be…* were just some of the colorful signs hanging from rafters and on walls. The mirror-tiled ball over the huge dance floor began spinning and colored lights brought the party atmosphere alive. The band on the dais in the back of the room began playing standards from the fifties and the party was on. An exuberant Charlie, replete in hot pink poodle skirt and frilly white blouse came running through the crowd and up in her daddy's arms. "Do you like my poodle? Emma said it was the best costume ever. And look at my shoes?" She showed off one foot that had a white saddle oxford on it with bright, pink glitter shoelaces.

"I see. You are indeed the prettiest girl here. You going to save a dance for your old dad later?"

"Maybe! Put me down, Daddy. I want to show Granny my poodle." He did so and she was off like a streak through the laughing crowd.

Cole turned and caught a glimpse of Emma moving through the crowd toward one of the tables filled with platters of food. He headed in her direction but soon found himself hailed and stopped numerous times by townspeople and friends. When he next looked up, he caught site of her heading toward the band on the dais. He tried to intercept her, but he lost sight of her.

Darcy was instructing a young helper on placing more cups on the punch table when he finally extricated himself from the mayor and his family. "Darcy, have you seen Emma?"

"I think I saw her last headed into the kitchen. She wanted to check on the cake. Or did she go to the gift table? She's all over the place. I told her we had plenty of help covering everything, but you know her. Wasn't this a grand idea of hers? I can't believe you pulled off such a surprise. And it's so much fun that most of the guests came dressed in the clothing of the 1950s."

"It's amazing, alright. Had no idea so many people could actually keep a secret around here." He laughed in return.

His eyes were still seeking out the hostess of the evening. Cole finally caught up with her coming out of the kitchen double doors while he was going in through them. He caught her wrist and she had no recourse but to follow him as he turned around and sought out a semi-quiet spot in the corner of the room.

"Cole, I was going to check—"

"There are plenty of people doing that already. Darcy said so. Between her crew and the ladies from the church auxiliary and the garden club and more… you can be spared to enjoy some of the party you put together. So, relax, Emma, and have some fun. There's a dance floor out there somewhere under this crowd and I figure we need to make use of it," he said, a wide grin underscoring his words.

"I'm not a good dance partner," she replied, a half-smile on her face as she shook her head. "I barely can do a two-step and certainly not the twist or jive or whatever it is they're doing out there."

"Well, neither can most of the people here. They could once, but I think they've toned things down a little due to the age group." They laughed at that statement. "That means we'll seem like experts in comparison. I know some steps and I'll teach you."

"Well… I guess…" Her words were cut off by the drum roll and the band leader asking people for silence.

He was introducing the guests of honor for the evening. Cole pulled Emma along through the crowd that was gathering closer to the stage.

"I'm not one for making speeches as you all know." Vernon was leading off. "I leave all the talking to my wife." That brought a thunderous roar from the crowd and soft swat on the shoulder from the woman beside him. "But all I have to say is that for fifty years, this woman saw fit to put up with me through good, bad, and in-between. And I hope she'll agree to another fifty because we ain't done yet." He grinned at Mae and then he leaned down and gave her a kiss before all gathered there. That brought more loud hoots and clapping. Mae's cheeks glowed almost as pink as Charlie's poodle skirt. It was her turn at the microphone.

"Y'all don't know how much this means to us to have all of you with us tonight. This was a surprise and then some. And I know that it was due in large part to a young lady who came to the rescue of Charlie and me one cold evening a few months back. We managed to talk her into staying around in our town for a bit. It seems like she was born here and we can't imagine not having her here for a lot longer. Where's Emma Cramer?" She held up her hand over her eyes trying to block the glare of the spotlights and find the person she sought.

The crowd helped her out and a push from Cole had her in front of the group. She kept a firm grip on the hand that she held of his.

Mae sent her a huge smile and her hand went to her heart in a sincere gesture. "You are a beautiful angel that came our way when we most needed one. You have our hearts and thank you for making this night one we will cherish forever."

A napkin appeared just as Emma needed one to stem the tears that appeared without warning. "She speaks for all us," Cole whispered the words next to her ear as he dipped his head. "I'm finding myself giving thanks more each day to those angels, too."

Mae and Vernon reached her side and Emma found herself wrapped inside Mae's hug. "I meant every word, young lady. You've given me so much to be happy about in such a short time. No words can tell you how much."

Vernon nodded beside her. "Ditto on that for me, young lady. You also have the makings of a fine mechanic... with a few more lessons. I might even let you take a turn or two on that combine when the crops are ready. I've seen you eyeing it a time or two."

Emma laughed, drying away the tears. "That's a deal."

The photographer came up at that moment. "Let's get you all together for a few photos and then you can get back to your party." Moving to the side of the dance floor, he had Mae seated in a chair, and then placed Vernon behind her. Then the next, he added Cole beside his father and Charlie standing next to Mae. Emma smiled at the group of people she had come to love in such a short amount of time. Then Mae was motioning to her. Emma shook her head and took a step back.

Cole was fast on his feet. He saw her retreating. He caught her wrist and drew her into the arrangement. She was between the two men. Mae beamed at her. "That is perfect, Emma. Did you think you would escape us?"

"I'm not one of the family... these are family photos, Mae."

"We took a vote and it was unanimous," Vernon surprised her when he spoke up, beaming a smile upon her. "You're family whether you like it or not. Now smile."

THOSE WORDS KEPT repeating in the back of Emma's mind over the next couple of hours. *It was unanimous.* Was that how they all felt? Cole, included? Or was she just being fanciful? When had that become a possibility in her mind? She was only looking for a temporary job... a way to help her gather some money and get on down the road. She had plans. What had happened to those?

"No frowns permitted tonight." Cole's words interrupted her thoughts. "If someone spiked the punch or they need more plates on the cake table... someone else is handling it. Smile, pretty lady... the next dance is ours."

Her hand was in its favored place—inside his—as he led her into the center of the floor. There were other couples around them, but funny how they disappeared when Cole's arms opened and she stepped inside them. The music began and Emma recognized it as one of her favorites.

Cole smiled down at her. "Now that is more like it. I hope you like the song I asked them to play. Thought it would be a nice change from all the rock-n-roll."

"'Blue Moon'... I love it." *And I love you.*

The words were on the tip of her tongue and she squelched them, her head moving to rest just beneath his broad shoulder. She was grateful she hadn't made a fool of herself just then. *Don't think. Just dream for a little while.* The lights dimmed and just the sparkles from the revolving mirror ball over their heads glittered around the room and over the dancers.

The song was slow and seductive and long. For that she was grateful. Eyes closed, her cheek resting where she could hear the beating of his heart beneath her ear. *Was it racing like hers?* How nice that would be. His arms tightened around her waist and her arms reached up, her hands entwining around his neck. She caught a glimpse of Mae smiling at them from the edge of the dance floor. Then she walked over and motioned for the band leader. Perhaps she had a request?

Emma put it from her mind and wanted to savor the last of the dance. It did seem to linger a bit. The song could play forever and she'd be happy to remain in their own little world. The music continued. However, all songs did end eventually. It seemed Cole was as reluctant as she to break the cocoon of their little world. Other couples disbursing around them brought reality back. His eyes glittered with an emotion that caused her pulses to race as his gaze met hers.

"That's our song, Emma Cramer."

"We have a song?" she whispered.

"Yes, we do. What do you think about that?" She had a feeling that it just wasn't a song he was talking about. This felt like one of those moments that she would remember the rest of her days.

"I like it."

"Me, too. We'll take a picnic lunch out tomorrow to the pond on the ranch. Just the two of us. I think there are some things we need to get around to discussing at last... barring any more interruptions or detours. Mom is already keeping Charlie. Think you can have a picnic basket ready when I get home... say four o'clock? There's a great place to watch the sunset from."

This was happening. Emma's life was about to take one of those unplanned detours. It would either be a hell of a ride or a dead-end road. Either way, her future would be set tomorrow, one way or another.

"Sounds like a plan."

A FEW MINUTES after their dance, while Emma was still basking in the glow of all things possible, and Cole was standing with his back turned to her while he listened to a couple who had stopped to speak with him. She saw Cole reach for his phone. A minute or so later, there was something about his shoulders... they seemed to gain a rigid set to them. Emma *sensed* a change.

She couldn't see all his face as he turned to where he was in silhouette, his eyes seeming to search out his parents across the floor. There was a tightening she noted along his jawline. He wasn't supposed to be on call that evening. Had that changed? He finished the call and instead of heading in her direction, he went in the opposite. She lost sight of him among the crowd. *Odd.*

Charlie raced up at that moment and drew her attention. "Can I have one more piece of Granny and Gramps' cake?"

"Don't you think you've had enough sweets for this evening? I think maybe one cookie and that is it. There will be more than enough cake left for you to have a piece tomorrow after your lunch. Deal?"

Charlie tried giving that "poor little me" look that served her so well in the past, but it didn't work. "Cookie now and cake tomorrow... or neither?" Emma stood firm.

Charlie finally changed expression to one of resignation. "Okay. A cookie now."

Emma took her hand and they headed toward the sweets table. "I do thank you for asking first, Charlie. You are really using good manners this evening. I know your granny and gramps think you are being a super good girl at their party."

That brought the wide grin back to the child's face. She

skipped along a bit beside Emma. Then a thought struck her. "Tomorrow... are we still getting the tree? And can we get the angel? Please?"

Emma almost had forgotten the plan. "I think the plan was to get the tree on Sunday after church. But I think we could make a trip to Dryden's Department Store and find that angel tomorrow. After chores are done in the morning, we can do that. Maybe even have lunch at the diner with Darcy. Sound like a plan?"

"That's the best plan. I wish tomorrow was here already. I love you, Emma."

Four simple little words, spoken so matter-of-factly, but they rocked Emma's world to the core. She missed a step and Charlie gave her a look.

"Did you hit your foot on something?"

"No. I guess I just need to look where I'm going. You choose the cookie you want." They had arrived at the table.

Emma watched the child examine the trays for the one perfect last cookie of the evening. All the while, her heart was squeezing in her chest. She had heard the heartfelt sentiment from three of the four members of the Drayton family in the space of the last few hours. That left a fourth member to weigh in and he was nowhere in sight. But tomorrow... Cole had promised *tomorrow* would be their time. Perhaps the words she longed to hear would come tomorrow and it would indeed be unanimous in her heart. She joined Charlie in hoping tomorrow would hurry up and come.

Chapter Twelve

Emma paused outside Cole's bedroom door. She listened and heard no sounds. Perhaps he was already downstairs? Vernon and Mae had driven them home last evening after the party... she and Charlie. After the phone call had come, Cole had appeared a few minutes later beside the trio. His expression gave nothing away. But Emma could tell there was something that had changed. She couldn't place her finger on it, but it was there.

She hoped the news hadn't been something horrific that he had to deal with for his job. He had simply said he might be very late and had left them, after insuring Vernon would see them all home. He hadn't made eye contact with Emma and the thought kept flitting through her mind all the way home and even as she had put Charlie to bed and then sat in the kitchen another hour until she could no longer keep her eyes open.

Today was the day she and Cole would finally have their time together. He had promised... a picnic for just the two of them and then... who knew what would happen for them all by the end of the day? She knew in her heart what her hopes were. But years of having hopes and dreams dashed for one reason or another, had taught her to be cautious. *Still…* Cole never made promises he didn't keep. She knew that about the man. His word was his bond and she would trust in that.

Emma stepped out onto the back porch, her eyes taking in the fact that Cole's SUV was nowhere in sight. Had he come in very late and already left again? Or had he not come in at all? A sliver of fear ran through the back of her mind and she beat it down. If there was anything bad, she would have heard from Vernon or Mae or any number of people before then. *Think positive.*

She went about the routine of breakfast for her and Charlie, but she did keep an extra plate of food in the warmer… *just in case* the backdoor opened and Cole came in. Charlie came downstairs, already dressed in blue and white overalls and a dark blue turtleneck. One shoe was tied and one wasn't. Angel scooted ahead of her and Emma held the door for her to escape into the backyard. Charlie laid her hair ties beside her plate for Emma to use for the pigtails she wanted to wear for the day. It was clear she wanted to waste no time getting their day started. Emma smiled; she knew her own anticipation for the day ahead.

"Is Daddy coming to the angel store with us?" She asked between bites of toast.

"I don't know. He's working on something at his office. He may be later this afternoon. Unless you want to wait for another day to—"

"Pleeease no, it needs to be today. I want the angel ready for the tree."

"Okay. It will be today as promised. Did you get your bed made?"

She nodded and finished the last of her milk. "I just need you to help with my hair. Can we do pigtails?"

Emma smiled. Her assumption was correct. "Pigtails it will be. Let's load the dishwasher and then we'll get to it."

Emma had to stifle a grin or two over the next hour. The child didn't even have to be asked or reminded what needed to be done to get the morning chores completed and in record time. Emma soon put Charlie out of her silent misery. Braiding the hair and getting her jacket on her and buttoned, they left Angel in charge of the house and were headed toward town at last.

Her cell phone rang and she saw Cole's name. Pulling over to the side of the road, she answered when normally she would have allowed it to go to voicemail for later.

"Hello?"

"It's Cole," he said, without preamble. "I'm sorry I haven't been in touch before now. Things… well things are busy right now. I just wanted to check in so you wouldn't be worrying or anything."

He sounded strange. She didn't want to get into a lengthy conversation with Charlie's big ears in the car. But Emma couldn't help being concerned.

"I understand. Your job has times like this. I'm just glad to hear from you. We're on our way to pick up Charlie's angel. Do you want to meet us at the store?"

There was a pause. "I'm afraid I can't do that. I'm out in the field right now. I may be tied up the rest of the day. I really don't know when I'll make it home. Tell Emma I'm sorry. And I'm sorry about our picnic. I wish I had time to explain more, but I really have to go right now. You two take care, okay?"

"Of course. You do the same." She wasn't sure he heard the last of her words before he had disconnected from the call.

Emma was more confused and concerned than before. Cole didn't sound like himself. He must have a lot on his mind and she needed to remember such was the life of a lawman and she needed to be able to handle that… if things progressed as she had dared hope. But now that their picnic was on hold, she found that little niggling feeling of doubt creeping in. *No!* She refused to let it ruin the day at hand.

"Your daddy can't meet us, but he said that he knows you will pick out the most perfect angel for the tree. He can hardly wait to see it." She smiled at the grinning child in the backseat, their eyes meeting in the rearview mirror. "Let's go find that angel for your big tree."

Dryden's Department Store was busy on the Saturday afternoon. They didn't find what pleased Charlie there. So, they moved on. They were passing a small secondhand store when Charlie stopped and stared in the window. Suddenly, Emma found her hand being pulled in the direction of the door of the shop.

"Where are we going?"

"I found her! She's so beautiful!"

And Emma had to admit that the angel in its box on the display shelf was indeed beautiful with her feathered wings and bright blue eyes dressed in a gown of rich golds and burgundies. Charlie's gaze was mesmerized on the angel. Emma paid for the item and Charlie watched the salesperson box it and get it ready to go home with her. Emma looked over the surrounding shelves, and allowed her gaze to check the scene outside the store through the large windows where she had come to stand.

It was a typical Saturday afternoon in McKenna Springs. There was traffic with all the locals coming into town from the area ranches for shopping and the tourists from Austin and surrounding places taking advantage of the variety of specialty shops around the town square that made the town such a favorite place for weekend jaunts. Emma glanced at her watch and made note that the diner at the opposite corner of the street had a few patrons coming and going after the lunch hour was past. That would be their next stop after the purchase of the angel. She was about to turn away from the window when a familiar figure caught her eye.

Cole came around the corner of the bookstore on the opposite corner and then stopped. He glanced at the car that had pulled into the parking spot in front of where he stood. Perhaps she should text and get his attention to let him know where they were and he could join them? Then that train of thought stopped dead in its tracks. Pretty much the same as Emma's breathing did as she stood transfixed on what was going on across from her vantage point.

From the car, a woman had exited. She had long golden hair down her back and it swayed with the rest of the seductive moves of a body dressed in very classy dark green fitted jacket and slacks. She looked like money and very definitely not someone Emma guessed came from McKenna Springs. At least she had not seen her before and she would have remembered her. Expecting to see the woman extend a hand to Cole for a handshake perhaps… she was stunned when the woman, without missing a beat, stepped right up and into his arms and molded herself against his length… in broad daylight, in front of the world. She acted like it was the most natural… and practiced… greeting between them. The fact that Cole did not move away was not lost on Emma.

Nor did she forget the conversation where he told her he was out of the office… *in the field… too busy.* The words mocked her. She should turn away but she couldn't. It was sort of like watching a train wreck… one knew it was going to happen and be bad but they're drawn in. She continued to stand there as the couple separated, and Cole held the door for her to get back into the driver's seat of the sleek vehicle.

He rounded the car and slid into the passenger seat in a quick movement. Was he trying to not be seen? He had failed.

Don't jump to assumptions. It could be an old friend from college? A family friend? A *really* good family friend... her mind was in fragments. Charlie's voice brought her back to the inside of the store.

"Isn't she perfect?"

Emma turned and tried to focus her mind and gaze on the angel in Charlie's hands. The angel was beautiful... like the woman across the street. Whoever she was, she intruded on the moment and Emma didn't want that.

She smiled and nodded, giving the child back the box. "She is indeed. I think it's lunchtime. I'm starving... how about you?" She put on a happy face and kept it there. Good thing no one could see what her brain was doing.

They crossed the street to the diner and just before going inside, Emma typed a text... to Cole.

'Have angel. Going to grab lunch at diner. Can you join us?'

She waited and nothing. They went inside and waved to Darcy standing at the register, helping a customer. Charlie selected a seat at the far end of the counter. She liked sitting on the bar stools that could turn. While they considered the menu, a text came across Emma's phone. She looked at it. Cole had replied.

'Still out in field. Busy for few hours. Have fun. Glad you found angel.'

"Well, that has to be a bad news face if I ever saw one." Darcy's words were just above a whisper so Charlie wouldn't be distracted from showing her angel in its box to the other two waitresses. Emma met her concerned gaze.

"It's... nothing. Just my mind wandering off. It's been a busy morning."

"Don't think I buy that." Darcy smiled, speaking in a more normal voice. "But we'll discuss your lunch needs first. What can I get you two ladies?"

How about Cole and the truth? Those words felt like they wanted to be shouted out, but Emma swallowed them and went through the routine of helping Charlie decide on the grilled cheese sandwich and chips with chocolate milk shake. After all it was a special day... Charlie had her angel and she was happy. Emma had a dose of reality... *before it was too late*. There would be no picnic. At least not one with *her*.

Emma's appetite was gone. She pushed the salad around on her plate and only managed a couple of bites of the slice of apple pie Darcy insisted she try. The food was tasteless as far as Emma was concerned. She was aware of only two things... Cole had lied to her, and he was with a mysterious and beautiful woman while she sat with his daughter, feeling like all kinds of a fool. *That's what you get when you believe in foolish possibilities.*

Her phone rang. It was Mae. She excused herself from

the conversation Darcy was having with Charlie about Christmas lists and such to answer.

"Hi, Mae."

"I'm glad I got you, Emma. I wanted to let you know there's been a change of plans. Cole is going to be busy for the rest of today and probably late into the evening. He just phoned us. The overnight with Charlie will have to wait. I don't know if you've talked to him or not. He said he might not have time to call you also. I thought I would help him out and call for him. Hope you weren't already on your way or anything."

Was it her imagination or was Mae sounding a bit off today, as well? Maybe her brain was just coloring all conversations now with the Drayton family members? She was being silly. Or was she?

"That's fine, Mae. I understand. Charlie and I have things we can do to keep us busy. We might stop by on our way home later from town."

"Oh…well, we might not be here. We have some errands to run… for the farm and all. So, I wouldn't want you to make the trip for nothing. We'll probably see you at church tomorrow. Give Charlie a big hug for me. I'll call when I can." She hung up.

What was going on? Had the world suddenly gone off its axis? *Probably see us at church*? Mae Drayton had not missed a Sunday in the last eighteen years. She was proud of sharing that information with people. Emma was more confused than ever.

"I'm taking in the new Disney movie at the mall in Austin tonight. I have a couple extra tickets since the girls here can't go... they have dates or some such." Darcy grinned and nodded at the pair of young girls. "How about let's make a movie night of it?" Darcy smiled at Charlie and then at Emma. Emma had a feeling Darcy had been a mind-reader in another life... she was too good at knowing things. *A movie?* It certainly beat sitting in the house and letting her mind imagine all sorts of things that would only hurt worse. It wasn't like there was going to be a better offer made. She wasn't about to be sitting and waiting for whenever Cole Drayton made an appearance. She had made enough of a fool of herself over him.

"What about it, Charlie? Think we deserve to go out and have fun at the movies?" Emma smiled at the little girl who couldn't nod fast enough, braids flying around her head.

"Then, you have a date, Miss Darcy. We need some laughs tonight."

THERE HAD BEEN no sign of Cole when they got home after the movies. There had been one simple reply to her text letting him know where they would be... if he cared. *'Thanks. Have fun.'*

Emma had thrown her phone across the room when she read it. She hadn't turned the phone back on the rest of the evening. The night was long... with tossing and turning... and she felt horrible the next morning. She didn't know if Cole was home or not. And she made the decision that she and Charlie, who was slow to get moving that morning too, would stay home and not make the trip into town for church.

However, she needed to keep smiling for Charlie's sake. And her mind needed to get a handle on things for when Cole did show up again. She had just put away the lunch items, cleaned the kitchen and was pushing Charlie on her swing set when the familiar white SUV pulled into the driveway and parked. She kept her attention on the child. Until Charlie jumped from the swing and ran towards the tall figure who exited the car.

"Daddy! You're home! Wait till you see the angel we got." She laughed when he swung her up in his arms and rested her on his hip. Emma felt his gaze on her but she kept hers on picking up the dog toys that were strewn in the yard. She dumped them inside the box by the backdoor. She was aware Cole had stopped a couple feet away and returned Charlie to her feet.

"Why don't you run get the angel and I'll look at it in the living room in a few minutes. Emma and I need to have a grown-up talk right now."

Charlie knew that meant she wasn't supposed to listen so she ran up the steps. "Okay, Daddy. But you and Emma need to hurry."

He waited a moment or two after the door closed behind her.

"Are you going to look at me while I apologize or just keep ignoring me?" His voice was low and it hurt a spot inside her chest.

She loved the sound of it but that just made it hurt today for some reason. She kept her face in a noncommittal mask. She knew how to do that from years of practice. *Show them no tears.*

"No apologies are necessary. You were busy. Your work comes first. I hope everything is okay now."

"I don't know if everything will ever be okay again or not." His reply caught her off guard.

It was cryptic and his tone had grown weary. It struck a chord of compassion that still lurked inside her for him.

"Are you hungry? Have you eaten? I can fix something for you. Or maybe you just need some sleep."

"Thanks, sleep would be good, but I don't have time for it. I did catch a few winks at Mom's earlier, but not much. I don't have time for a meal. I just wanted to stop by for a few minutes and apologize and change clothes. And say I'm sorry that our plans for the picnic had to be put on hold."

"It's not a big deal. Charlie's happy with her angel."

Cole looked like he had the weight of the world on his shoulders. Was he feeling some remorse for the obvious lies he had told her about his day and whereabouts? She couldn't cut him much compassion in that area.

"She's back."

The words came out of his mouth and Emma wasn't certain at first that she had heard right.

Then he continued. "*Pamela*... my ex-wife is back in McKenna Springs. She showed up unexpectedly on the night of Mom and Dad's party. That was the phone call I received. She was at the office asking for me. Since then, I've been trying to find out why she came here and what she's up to."

"I see. And your mom and dad? Do they know? Is your brother here?"

"No, Jimmy isn't here. Seems they parted ways a while back. He took off to be some hunting guide in Alaska."

Emma had to ask. "What about Charlie? Did she say anything about her?"

Cole nodded slowly. "She wants to see her."

"Oh, no." Emma glanced toward the house where somewhere inside a happy little girl was oblivious as to what could impact her world. "Are you going to allow that?"

"I have no idea right now what I'm going to do about anything. Two days ago made sense. Then everything changed with a phone call. I'm meeting with my attorney in an hour. Mom and Dad are going to be there. I must try to get on top of all this. Until we get a better understanding of what's going on, I'm going to rely on you to keep things as normal as possible for Charlie. She has no idea of Pamela and for now, that's the way it needs to stay. She's our main concern."

"That goes without saying. And I'll do my best here so you all can concentrate on what needs to be done. Don't worry about anything here. I've got it." The only thing important at the moment was Charlie and Emma was determined to keep her world as drama-free as long as she could.

For the first time since he approached her, a smile curved the corners of his mouth.

There was warmth in his gaze and his words came with heartfelt sincerity. "I know and I can't express my gratitude for that enough. I don't know how much I'll be here over the next couple of days… or until this is all resolved."

"No problem. You do what you need to do and don't worry about anything else."

"Daddy, are you done talking yet?" Charlie's voice was more a plea than question. She saw the apology in his eyes sent her way before he answered the child. "Yes, I'm coming. Let's see this incredible angel."

Once Cole had pronounced Charlie's choice to be awesome, he had taken a quick shower and changed and was headed down the drive within a half-hour. Charlie stood at the door watching him leave and Emma was behind her.

"I wish Daddy didn't have to work so much."

Emma stroked the child's hair that fell down her back. "He has to help keep people safe and sometimes that takes more time. He'll be back as soon as he can. In the meantime, I promised him that you and I would keep things running just fine here. Okay?"

Charlie nodded. "Can we get the tree still?"

"I think we can do that. We're smart and can figure it out, right?"

"Yes, we can."

A Christmas tree hunt was just the thing to channel an almost six-year-old's attention into happy things… and to keep Emma's mind from unsettling thoughts and doubts of the future that had become murky at best.

Chapter Thirteen

"You two ladies certainly picked a honey of a tree. One of the biggest and best-shaped ones on the lot." Trish Wellman commented as Emma paid for their purchase.

She was ready to get the tree home and be done with their excursion. Charlie choosing a tree could have gone on for hours. Emma finally stepped in and had Charlie narrowed down to three. Then the final selection had been made and Emma quickly had the tree tagged for delivery the next day and had paid for it.

"I'm getting her off this lot before she changes her mind again. Thanks so much for helping two novices."

"It was fun. I'm sorry Cole couldn't be here. But he'll get the enjoyment of putting it up. Do come by the store if you need anything else."

"Thanks, we will." Emma walked out of the office and expected to see Charlie on the bench where she left her while she paid.

She looked around. She was on the verge of panic but not there at that moment. *Think*. She was probably looking at the tree again. She turned and headed in the direction of the row the tree was on, her heart beating faster with each step. Then she saw her... or *them*. Charlie wasn't alone. She was standing by the tree and the blonde Emma had seen with Cole the day before was bent down, speaking to Charlie. A fierce stab of protectiveness made Emma fly across the space, putting herself between Charlie and the woman. One hand got a firm grip on Charlie's hand.

She fixed the woman with a steady gaze. She meant to deliver a silent warning and the woman got the message, backing up a couple of steps. "Charlie, I told you to wait on the bench."

Even as she spoke to the child, her eyes did not leave the female in front of her.

"I'm afraid that's my fault. I asked if she had chosen a tree and she said yes and how beautiful it was. I asked if she'd show me. I'm sorry."

Emma heard the words, but she didn't buy into them. Pamela's eyes had a glint of insincerity behind their gaze. She said the right things and smiled correctly with contrite body language... but Emma sensed it was all a show. And she was clearly expected to be stupid enough to buy into it. The most important information she kept to herself and that was the fact Emma knew her identity. But Charlie didn't. And she intended to keep it that way until the Drayton's said otherwise.

"You're a stranger and Charlie knows better. They have

people here who can help you with a tree, if you need one. Let's go, Charlie."

Emma didn't stop and kept her hold firm on Charlie. "Are you mad at me, Emma?"

"No, Charlie, I was just very worried when you weren't on the bench. But you need to remember the rule about talking to strangers." She didn't stop until she had Charlie in the car and they were on the road toward the ranch.

Charlie was quiet for a few minutes. "I'm sorry, Emma. I promise I won't do that again."

Emma gave her a smile in the rearview mirror before returning her attention to the road. "I'll hold you to that promise, sweetie. We just want you to always be safe and happy. Now what about hamburgers for dinner? I think we might try to make them ourselves on the grill. Good idea?"

"Fun! Yes, I want to make outdoor hamburgers."

Not only did they make hamburgers, but Emma had brought out reams of construction paper, glue and glitter. The dining room table had been covered in plastic sheeting and became their "studio". She showed Charlie how to make garlands of red and green paper chains and white paper became intricate, lacy-looking snowflakes. Charlie was enthralled. Emma was the official cutting person and Charlie became queen of the glitter bottles. There was much laughter and that was what was needed at the moment. It helped the hours pass quickly.

"Let's place our finished garlands and hanging snowflakes in this plastic container I found in the basement. Then we'll carefully roll up the plastic from the table and floor and dump it in the trash can out back." Emma handed the bottles of glitter to Charlie to place in the smaller box they found in the kitchen pantry.

"Can we bake cookies for my class? In those different shapes like trees and—" Charlie's sentence was interrupted by the sudden low growl coming from Angel.

Emma and she stopped still, both amazed and shocked, to hear such a surprising sound coming from the little dog. Emma looked under the table where the dog had been lying so quietly at their feet as they worked. Warning bells sounded in her brain as she saw that Angel was standing on all fours, the ruff of fur standing stiff around her neck... her gaze zoned in on the direction of the front door. Very few people ever used the front door of the house. Most people visiting just came through the back door. Without conscious thought, Emma stepped to the backdoor and turned the dead bolt. Then she spoke in a pleasant, but quieter voice to Charlie.

"I need you to go upstairs and find the pink plastic bag inside my closet and then gather all the crayons you can find in your room and place them inside it. We'll need those for our next project tomorrow."

Charlie was quickly on her way, happy with thoughts of what they would create next. Emma knew the pink bag would take a while for her to find as it was really under her bed, but Charlie wouldn't stop hunting until she found it. Her hand went to the dimmer switch and she lowered the lights in the dining room. There were no lights on in the living room and she was grateful for that. The plantation blinds were drawn as was her habit in the evenings. Moving around Angel, who still maintained a steady bead on the front door, she tiptoed to the hall closet and quickly opened the safe on the shelf that was level with her eyes. The first day of her arrival, both Mae and Cole had shown her where the place was and the combination needed to retrieve the small loaded pistol from inside.

Emma hated guns, but she was grateful there was one she could use if needed. Her heart jumped several beats when, through a slit in the blinds at the window in the hallway, she saw the automatic motion lights come on at the side of the house. Something… or someone… was moving along the sidewalk around the corner of the porch. Angel advanced in a slow-motion stance that made Emma's fear compound. Dogs knew when danger was near… more so than their human counterparts. Taking the gun in hand, she moved to the table next to the front door, placing it on the tabletop behind a flower arrangement… concealed if Charlie came into the room, but close enough where Emma could grab it if needed.

She drew out her cell phone from her pocket. Her first thought was to call the sheriff's department. But what if it were only an animal? A deer possibly? She'd waste their time and alarm a lot of people with an emergency call to the sheriff's home. She wanted to call Cole. But he had enough to deal with and, again, what if it was nothing? She had promised him that she would handle things at home so he could concentrate on the Pamela issue.

Vernon. She'd call him. He was closer than anyone else to their location. She hit the speed dial button. The phone rang... and rang... and no answer. She ended the call and then typed in the text message they had agreed upon as their own equivalent of an emergency code... 321. She hit send and her heart stopped. There was a tapping at the front door. Angel emitted a loud bark, followed by the guttural growl.

Charlie appeared at the top of the stairs. "Is someone outside, Emma?"

Emma kept her voice steady and her gaze met Charlie's. "I need you to go to the special closet at the end of the hall and stay there until I come get you. Do you understand?"

The eyes grew wide in the child's face, but she just nodded and disappeared in a run. Emma waited until she heard the faint sound of the door closing upstairs. If people didn't know, and most didn't, only the immediate family and Emma did... in the hall closet, behind the winter coats and such, there was a smaller trap door that allowed a person to enter into a recess between the walls of the bedrooms. Charlie had been told it was an emergency safe place and only go there if told to do so or she was really scared. And never ask why if she was told to run there and stay. Thankfully, the child followed the instructions without issue.

The tapping came again, louder. Emma knew it was up to her to face whatever was on the other side of the door. She also needed to slow down everything as much as she could… to buy time for help to arrive. She drew in a deep breath. Charlie had to be kept safe, first and foremost. She glanced at Angel. The dog seemed to know she was the backup and moved to stand poised for a charge, beside Emma. "Okay, Angel. It's on us," she whispered in the heavy silence.

Take the offensive. She placed a determined look on her face, eyed the distance to the concealed gun, and then opened the door a couple of inches, her foot wedged against the back of it. Her voice was clear and steady, much to her surprise.

"What is it?" Her brain hit an imaginary speed bump that made her grab for the first words that she could find. Pamela Drayton stood on the porch, at the front door. *What in the world?*

"Hello. I'm sorry if I frightened anyone. And I know it's a bit late to be calling. But I don't know if you have heard of me or not and this—"

"I know who you are. Why are you here right now?"

Emma's response and direct gaze clearly gave the other woman pause. Emma felt something akin to anger and righteous indignation growing inside her. How dare this poor excuse for a mother appear in the dead of night at the home she forfeited any right to set foot in or around years ago... abandoning her own child and husband. Emma's grip tightened on the door handle.

Pamela's gaze took in the dog that had sidled closer to Emma's foot.

"Now aren't you a ferocious little one?"

"Looks are deceiving. Her teeth are just as sharp as a coyote's. She protects her own."

That brought the woman's green-eyed gaze back to meet Emma's. "I'm sure of it. You both seem to be ready to do just that. But I realize you're paid to babysit and all, but I can assure you that—"

"State your business."

The gaze narrowed and the smile left the woman's face. "I was just returning Cole's gloves." She raised her hand, showing the familiar pair of brown leather gloves. "I thought he might be missing them. He left them in our hotel room last night. He left so early this morning that he must have overlooked them."

Emma tried to deflect the words and their implications from her heart. Maybe it was just the woman's ploy to get under her skin? Or maybe Cole had succumbed to the charms that caught him the first time around with this woman? There were a lot of maybes forming in her mind. But then a calmness settled in place.

"I expect *you* can give them to him. One of the vehicles flying up the road behind you will be his." She soundly shut the door in the woman's face.

Her forehead leaned against the cool wood. Her ears picked up the sounds of the woman's booted feet moving from the doorway. The engines of the two SUVs she had spotted flying up the road from the front gate toward the house, one with light bars flashing, had been like the cavalry to the rescue and emboldened her to slam the door in the woman's face. She heard the vehicles come to a halt and then the sound of muted voices. She didn't care to hear what was being said. On autopilot, she reached for the gun and returned to the hall closet, stepping inside and opening the safe.

The door flew open and Cole was the first one inside. He saw her and advanced to the door. Concern was etched over his whole being.

"Is Charlie okay? Are you okay? Did she—"

"Yes, Charlie is okay and doesn't know anything except she got to go to the 'secret cave' and is waiting there until I come get her. I am fine. No, *your* Pamela did not enter this house. I did my job." She shut the gun away, locked the safe.

Then Emma shut the closet door behind her... all without setting her eyes on the lawman. She made it to the bottom of the stairs before his hand on top of hers on the balustrade halted her ascent and did bring her gaze to his.

"*Are* you okay, Emma? Why are you acting this way?"

"How am I supposed to act? My main concern was for Charlie and whatever danger there might be for her. I don't know anything that is going on with that woman and until I am told otherwise, I will continue to shield Charlie from her. I am doing the best I know how to do under the circumstances. Now, I need to get your daughter out of the hiding place and then you can spare a few minutes, I am sure, to try to explain whatever you need to her. But I will also tell you, that Pamela approached Charlie at the tree lot earlier today. I called your office to speak to you about it when we got home earlier but they said you were out. This wasn't a random visit tonight. Apparently, after you two spent the night together last night and you left your gloves behind, she felt she had the right to come to your house. The rest, you can sort out. It's none of my business."

Cole didn't stop her and for that she was grateful, reaching the hall closet and then tapping on the little door. The little girl shot out of the hiding spot and locked her arms around Emma's neck in a tight grip.

Emma sank down on the flooring and held her for several long moments, stroking her hair. "It's okay, little one. Your daddy and grampy are downstairs and Angel, too. All is safe and good. I'm proud of you for doing what you were told to do. You are such a smart, brave girl."

"Daddy's here?" The reply was muffled against Emma's shoulder.

"Yes, I'm here, princess." Cole had approached the pair quietly and waited.

He had just enough time to brace himself before Charlie flew out of Emma's arms and into his. He stood and gathered the child closer. Emma rose more slowly and paused in the doorway of the child's room. Cole sat on the edge of the frilly bed and Charlie continued to hold on to him.

"Just like Emma said, you did everything you were supposed to do and I am so very proud of you. But all is safe and sound here in your house… thanks to Emma and Angel. You truly do have two of the best guardian angels watching over you." Cole met Emma's gaze above the child's head.

His silent gratitude should have warmed her heart… *should have*. Her heart was a bit busy hoisting a familiar wall into place once again. Gratitude was not love. And Emma needed to realize the difference. If anything, the night's events had removed the silly rose-colored glasses she had hid her common sense behind the last few months. This was a job. These people were not her family. They were her employers… *period*.

"You look tired, Emma. I've got her. I'll put her to bed. You need to get some rest."

Cole's words spurred her to move. "Goodnight." Emma didn't pause until she was inside her room and shut the door.

She didn't even turn on the lights. Curling up into a fetal position on top of her bed covers, she shut her eyes… squeezing them to stay shut as moisture built up and then escaped from beneath her lashes. She hated the pain that came with caring too much. She tried to keep it away and had done well… until coming to McKenna Springs and making the mistake of staying. *Staying*… she had even fooled herself into thinking she could actually stay and be happy here. *Stupid fool.* She berated herself for the weakness and allowing the pain to reach her heart.

Things were changing around her. The Draytons had much on their plates to deal with now. Maybe the return of Charlie's mother was a good thing. *Really?* Emma was biased in that regard. She had no idea how any mother could walk away from their child. And to throw away the love of a good man like Cole? The woman had it all at one time... and it wasn't good enough then, why would it be different now?

Maybe she had some epiphany and was a changed woman, seeking a second chance and forgiveness? Emma tried to find an ounce of forgiveness for her, but it wouldn't come. She was too close to it all. And that was when a granule of truth began to grow into a real seed. *She was too close.* She needed to give them all a chance to allow whatever change that was meant to be to happen. Looking up at the dark ceiling, the invisible writing was on it. There was only one question in need of an answer. Was she brave enough to reveal it?

Chapter Fourteen

"I WAS GOING to let you sleep a bit longer before I disturbed you for breakfast." Mae's words met her as Emma came into the kitchen. Her quick glance around the room told her that the two women were alone. No sign of Charlie... or of Cole. Although she had steeled herself to not be surprised if that was the case. It had become the "new" normal of late. Cole was a busy man... a sheriff, a rancher, a father, and a man with his beautiful "ex" wanting back in his life. *Yes, he was a busy man.*

"I'm glad you can still attempt a smile even after last night. When Vernon received your emergency text, he was out of that office like a shot from a cannon, grabbing his rifle as he went. Cole wasn't far behind after his dad got him on the radio in the truck. They met up at the front gate to this place. Vernon gave me most of the story after he got home." She pushed a mug of coffee toward Emma and waited while she settled herself on one of the stools.

"I've got a short stack and sausage here," Mae said, adding the last pancake to the plate before setting it in front of Emma. "I can add eggs also. Fruit, maybe?" The woman was being kind and Emma had to fight to hang on to her resolve. She shook her head. "This is more than enough, thank you. And I feel like I need to be on that side and you should be sitting here. I'm not an invalid and it's my job."

Mae's brow knitted at the words but she didn't respond with the question that was clearly in her gaze. "Cole is at the office. Grampy took Charlie into town to school. Cole already had a word with the principal and teacher and there's someone going to be close by Charlie from now on. They won't get in your way and you probably won't know they are even around most of the time, but you won't be on your own as you were last night without someone to rely upon for help in a shorter response time."

Emma looked at the woman and took in the words. "Is Cole worried that Pamela may be up to something that could harm Charlie? I thought they were talking and things were going to be worked out."

"You know Cole. He doesn't leave things to chance. He would rather err through an abundance of caution than through not being prepared in advance. I know this is all confusing. And I told those two men of mine that they should have brought you into their thinking before now. It would have left you better prepared."

"Is that what you're doing now? Preparing me?" Emma's gaze met Mae's.

The older woman gave a smile and slow nod.

"You are a smart girl, Emma. Smarter than you've been

given credit for. And I can't say how much it touched my heart when I heard how you reacted to protect Charlie last night. I felt before that you were sent to cross paths with us, but now I am sure of it. You came to us for a reason that day at the crossroads at the station. I firmly believe that. I don't think Charlie could ever be in a safer place than with you. I think you would have given your life to protect her… and that is something I will never forget. Cole knows that, too. I hope you realize that."

"I'm doing my job to take care of her. I care for Charlie very much. Whatever is best for her is what I want."

Mae seemed to want to say more, but the words didn't come. She nodded and returned to placing the utensils and pans she had used earlier inside the dishwasher. If she had any comments about Emma's response or demeanor, she didn't voice them.

"WHATEVER YOU MEN are going to do about this situation, you best get it done. This threat of impending doom hanging over our heads is getting to everyone." Mae's words preceded her into Cole's office where Vernon and two other men were seated around the conference table in the corner. Cole stood and drew another chair up next to him for his mother to take a seat and join them.

"That's what we're discussing," Vernon replied.

"Enough discussion. What are we going to *do* about all this?"

"Did you speak with Emma... about the added protection?"

Mae's gaze zeroed in on her son. "Yes, *I* did speak with her this morning. And she understood. She's a lot smarter than she's been given credit for. That woman was ready to do battle with whatever was outside that door last night... with any weapons necessary... including a brain that can far outshine *some* of the ones at this table. I spoke with her... something *you* should be doing instead."

Cole drew his gaze away after receiving his mother's message loud and clear. "Paul, Davis... thank you both for meeting with us this morning. I'll look over those papers, Paul, and get them back to your legal secretary this afternoon. Davis, I appreciate the loan of one of your trusted officers taking this assignment on while off the official clock."

"You've been there a time or two to help me out," the ranger spoke up, rising and taking his hat off the rack by the door. "We won't let anyone harm your two ladies... Charlie and Emma are special to a lot of us, too." Cole nodded and the fact Davis indicated that he understood Emma was a vital part of any equation involving Cole put an added ease to Cole's mind. The door shut behind the two men.

"You just called a ranger and our attorney less than bright," Vernon said, his head shaking as he looked across at his wife.

"I didn't just call *them* less than bright. You and our son are *also* in this room." Mae never was one to mince words.

Cole was the referee. "We should have handled things better. Hindsight is twenty-twenty. But we're getting to a resolution. The question is whether we can all live with it or not?"

Vernon nodded. Mae's gaze grew concerned as she looked at her son. "I'm more than a little concerned. I know where your dad and I stand on this. We back you up a hundred per cent. I know you've thought about Charlie in this situation. And I hope you've given some thought to Emma, also. You know how we feel about her."

"I couldn't help but know how you feel about Emma, Mother. And I have included her in all the scenarios I've grappled with over the last couple of days. Until this is all resolved, Charlie is the priority. I have to trust that Emma will understand."

"Let's hope we're making the right decision."

Cole only nodded his agreement to that statement as silence fell around the table.

EMMA WAS AWARE that normalcy was key in any child's daily routine. With Charlie being as precocious and smart as she was, she needed to keep ahead of the game and focus on keeping to the norm in the daily routine. It was hard at first, knowing they were being watched... and by whom, she did not know. But she trusted that the person was very good or Cole would not have entrusted his daughter's safety to them.

She hoped the person liked diner food. She had given in to Charlie's request to stop at the diner after school and get one of Darcy's pies to take home. And Emma felt the need to get her mind removed from the gloom filling it. Darcy was a good one to put smiles in place of frowns. She did so right away as Emma and Charlie stepped through the doorway. They had to return the warm greeting Darcy shot their way from behind the counter.

"Well, it's about time you two ladies show up. I've had bar stools reserved and you haven't been in here to take them. What'll you have now that you're here?"

"Pie please. A pecan one for my daddy. We're putting stuff on the tree tonight and he likes pecans."

Emma shook her head and grinned as Darcy shot her a look. "We're decorating the Christmas tree with ornaments tonight. Charlie thinks we need a special dinner to go along with it. It's a big occasion."

Darcy grinned at the little girl. "And so it is! And I bet your tree will be the best one in all the county. I've heard about the special decorations and all."

"Mae must have told you," Emma responded.

"It's a surprise. Emma and me are going to surprise daddy with the ones we made. There're some bought ones too, but I like ours the best."

"Emma and I, you mean."

"That's right. Emma and *I* are going to surprise Daddy." The child repeated with a grin at Emma's correction.

"One pecan pie coming up. And how do you like these new coloring sheets I got for my younger customers? Want to try one out?" Darcy pulled a sheet and a small box of crayons from beneath the counter and placed in front of the child. Charlie was clearly pleased by the turn of events.

"Coffee?" she asked Emma. "I'll get Joe to box up a pie for you."

"Just water with lemon, will be fine. Thanks, Darcy."

When she returned with the water glass, she gave Emma a look. "I heard about the excitement at your place. Quite a shock for all involved."

Emma knew Darcy was being careful in the presence of Charlie's big ears.

She took a sip of the water. "Some."

"We had a visitor in here, too. I didn't invite them to stay long."

Emma read that message loud and clear. "Good for you."

Joe brought the box out and handed over to Darcy. "Here is one special pie for your daddy." She smiled at Charlie.

Emma took the box and rose from the stool. "Thank Miss Darcy for the coloring page and for this delicious smelling pie. We need to get to your house and get ready."

They paid for the pie and smiled another goodbye at the woman. "Why the frown?" Joe asked as Darcy returned to the counter. "Just something that was said. Nothing really." Joe shrugged and returned to the kitchen.

Emma had always referred to the Drayton place as "home"... until just a few moments ago. It was a "house" now... that brought the frown. Darcy dismissed it with a shrug of the shoulders. She was misreading things.

HOME. IT FELT good to finally just take some time and walk into the kitchen that smelled of roast in the oven, Christmas songs playing softly from the stereo in the living room, and Angel wagging the scraggly tail in greeting. Somewhere, there would be two females that he couldn't wait to see. Cole had moved heaven and earth for this time out of his day... one late afternoon and evening where he could breathe and hopefully find some hint of normalcy in a world that was turned upside down outside the doors of his home.

"Are there any elves out and about? Am I all alone in this house?" His raised voice called out into the silence as he walked from the kitchen to the doorway of the living room... and then stopped. His gaze took in the entire room in a slow perusal.

The huge tree stood in the corner of the room, a few feet from the fireplace and hearth where a nice, warm fire had been lit. Bright red and green paper chains were draped around and in the branches of the tree. The same type of chains was looped from the top to the bottom of the staircase. White snowflakes, their glittered fronts and backs catching the light from the lamps, softly turned on their invisible tethers as they moved in the air currents of the room from in front of the windows and above his head as he stood in the doorway. Now he knew why there were little bits of glitter here and there in the kitchen and dining room he had seen earlier in the week. The elves had been at work.

"Surprise, Daddy!"

The voice came from the stairs where Charlie had crept down and was crouching ready to spring into the room. He laughed and caught her as she took the last step.

"Isn't it pretty? Emma cut the paper and I glued it and put glitter on it. And we're going to bake a lot of cookies too in all shapes. And we have to get the tree ready so the angel can go on top. But you need a ladder and—"

"Hold on, princess, not so fast. Take a breath."

The child made a show of doing just that. But it didn't slow her down much. "The ladder has to be tall to reach the top. And there's regular balls that Granny let us borrow from her tree, too. And lights, Daddy. We need lots of lights, 'cause Emma likes those."

"I see. So, I better get the ladder from the garage and get busy. And we need to put those lot of lights on first. Do I have my elf helpers?"

He turned and Emma was standing on the stairs a few feet away. She looked so good to him. He wanted to draw her into the circle of his arms, too. But he had some unfinished business and he wasn't too certain Emma would welcome his arms being anywhere near her now. He couldn't fault her for that. He had quite a few things to sort out in his personal life. *One step at a time.* His mother's advice filtered through his brain.

Impatience could only make things worse. It had to be enough to just drink in the sight of her. For the special occasion that Charlie had deemed the evening, the child had chosen a red velvet jumper with a cream satin blouse. There was a pretty red hair bow that had to have been the handiwork of the woman who had moved to stand on the bottom step, still watching the pair in silence.

Emma's long skirt in the same color of velvet was paired with cream-colored turtleneck in some fuzzy-textured material. He liked the fact her long hair was free and softly falling over her shoulders. She was beautiful and he tightened his grip on Charlie to keep his hands steady.

"Daddy, not so tight. Put me down so I can let Angel go outside before she helps us with the tree, too." He did as he was instructed.

"It's good to be here. You and Charlie picked a perfect tree." Was he making small talk in his own home? Would appear so.

"Thank you. It was all Charlie's choice on the tree. She

has a good eye for them. The Wellmans brought it out and she instructed them where to place it. You'll find the box of lights and ornaments in the corner. I'll see to dinner while the two of you get to work."

Something wasn't right. His hand shot out and covered hers before she could take another step from the stair. He hadn't meant to do it, but it was automatic. Making the simple connection with her hand was enough to send signals zooming throughout his body and his internal thermostat was in danger of serious overheating. *Steady.*

"We'll need your supervision, too." He took a moment and then continued. "I know things have been crazy around here and none of this I planned, but …"

"Please, don't apologize. More than enough people have apologized already. I really don't need it. Everything has turned out fine and Charlie is untouched. She'll have her tree and her angel and all will be well in her world… as it should be. That's what matters. You all need a good Christmas in this house. And if I don't check the roast, we may have to have just salad and that would ruin Charlie's plans." She withdrew her hand because she could.

His grip had eased. Another grip had taken hold. Emma sounded the same and she looked much the same… maybe a little darkness around her eyes, but the spark that was always lurking in her blue eyes wasn't visible when she looked at him. Had things changed that much? Or had he misread her before? Why couldn't things make sense like they did once?

Charlie came bounding back in the room and claimed his hand. "Let's go, Daddy. We can start before Emma calls us for dinner."

A COUPLE OF times, Emma had peeked into the living room. She had taken care not to disturb the scene before her. A smile filled her insides. Cole was on the stepladder intent on another string of lights going on the branches just right. Emma held part of the strand off the floor and helped when he need more lights to be freed. She was so intent on her job. Angel was right beside her, her attention on what her humans were doing. When a familiar Christmas song came on the stereo, with lyrics that Charlie knew, she joined in and after a bit, so did Cole. Emma froze the moment in her mind and then buried into a special place in her heart… it should have helped ease the constant ache that was there. It only seemed to heighten it so she tiptoed back to the kitchen.

The potatoes and carrots were ready to place into a dish. The roast came out of the oven and rolls went inside to brown. There was a tap at the backdoor and then the familiar voices.

"Are we late? Vernon got held up with one of the farm hands and a machinery issue." Mae came in ahead of the big man who had two covered dishes in his hands. He set them on the island and smiled at Emma. "I hear there's a pecan pie somewhere in the vicinity?"

Emma grinned. "And I suppose a little bird named Charlie let that out of the bag?"

Vernon clasped his hands. "That's my girls, you two did good today. My wife should take lessons."

"Get your coat off, old man, and see if your son needs help in the living room." Mae had already hung up her jacket in the mudroom. "It's going to freeze tonight. They even mentioned the word snow. We haven't had a good snow in three or four years now. But you never know nowadays… with all this climate change that's going on."

"I agree. And I'm just glad you both were able to come over on such short notice." Emma might have put the idea in Charlie's mind after they left the diner, but the child was eager to put the plan in motion. They had stopped by the Drayton's home on their way and given the invite. Emma thought it would be nice to have them all together for more reasons than one.

"We always enjoy spending time with our family. And you know that includes you in that word, also."

Emma kept her back to the woman and stayed busy with the relish dish. It was a couple moments before she managed to nod in a normal manner. "Could you check the rolls in the oven? I'll double-check the table." She took a little time in the dining room and then found her composure. Walking into the living room, she smiled. "Dinner will be on the table in five minutes. The rest of the trimming will have to pause while you all get washed up for the meal."

Charlie was out of the room in a flash. Vernon followed behind her. Cole hesitated beside the tree. "I need your opinion. Tell me if you think this is enough." He reached behind the tree and in a moment a blaze of colored lights illuminated the room.

Emma was speechless.

"Well..." He grinned. "Is it bad or good that you can't speak? Charlie said you liked a lot of lights so I put all I had on there. If you think it needs more I'll get more and—"

Emma drew in her bottom lip and tried to keep her smile normal as she shook her head. Words were hard to come by at first. Then she felt the knot move from her throat enough to speak. "I think it's perfect. I think it doesn't need anything else to make it beautiful just as it is. You and Charlie did a good job."

Cole moved to stand beside her, his gaze moving from her to the tree and then back to her. "Your first real tree needs to be special. I'm glad you and Charlie talked me into having this tree this year. It was the time to bring Christmas into this house in the proper way. Thank you, Emma."

The kiss was unexpected. She didn't have time to move. Maybe she didn't want to. Maybe she wanted this time, this moment to end on this note. *Don't wish for more. He's grateful. Accept his thanks and keep it in perspective.* It was hard to do that when every nerve in her body responded to his touch and his kiss made her want the fire and passion it invoked just as she needed air to breathe. That was the power a kiss from Cole Drayton wrought within her. She doubted she would ever feel as alive again as she felt with him. That sad realization made her step away. *Don't seek what isn't there.*

"I hope you're okay with my inviting your parents for dinner tonight. I thought it would make it special for Charlie." *And for you.* "Dinner is ready." She didn't wait for a response.

The confused look in his gaze was evident as she turned and left him.

Chapter Fifteen

"This pie was the perfect ending for a great meal. Good job, Emma." Vernon finished up the last crumb of pecan on his plate and made the comment with a satisfied smile on his face.

"I'll be sure and tell Darcy you said so. I wish I could bake pies like this."

"Now, Emma. Your cooking lessons will have to get back on track after the holidays. And we'll have you baking just as good as Darcy McKenna before spring. We might even enter you in the contest at the county fair. That should be a good goal." Mae's comment made Emma shake her head.

"I think you have delusions of grandeur that far surpass my skills, but thank you for the vote of confidence. I'll clear the table and the elves can continue their work in the living room. There'll be more pie and coffee for afterwards."

The kitchen was all but done when Charlie came in and took Emma by the hand. "You've got to come right now." Emma allowed herself, with Mae following, to be escorted into the living room.

Cole held out a box of ornaments that Mae had brought

over for the tree. "Pick one."

"Yes, pick one that's really pretty Emma. You must put the first ornament on the tree. Daddy put the lights on the tree. I'm putting the angel on the top. You have to put the first ornament." Charlie had it all worked out.

It touched Emma's heart that the child had wanted to give her such an important "job" on the special evening. Emma studied the box's contents. She chose a little porcelain blue bird.

"A bluebird on your tree brings happiness to all in the house. That's a most appropriate first ornament." Mae commented on the choice.

Emma chose a branch and stood on tiptoe to place it. *Bring them happiness, little bird. Please.* She stood back and Charlie clapped.

"Now we need to do a lot more." She carefully chose a shiny red ball next. They all got into the decorating and before long, the tree was pronounced complete. "The most perfect beautiful tree ever."

All except for one thing. Charlie carried the box from her room to the tree. Carefully, she lifted the angel in its gold gown, with gossamer wings and delicate features, from the tissue paper. Charlie bestowed a kiss on its head and then handed it over to Cole. He took the top step on the ladder. The angel was secured on the tallest spire of the tree. Charlie stood transfixed, her hands clasped under her chin. Emma smiled at the glow in the child's eyes.

"It really is the most beautiful tree ever. She's the best angel. She'll make this the bestest, most perfect Christmas. I know she will."

Mae glanced at Emma and Emma gave a slight shrug. It was enough that Charlie was happy.

"Did I hear something about another slice of pie earlier?" Vernon was already headed toward the kitchen.

Mae fell in right behind him. "Not another piece of that pie, mister. You've had enough."

"Oh, my!" The little girl looked round-eyed up at her father. "We forgot the stockings. There aren't any stockings here. They're at Granny's."

Cole considered the problem. He looked at Emma. "I don't think Santa would have a problem with there being stockings for the same person in two different locations. Do you?"

Emma seemed to give the matter some thought before she replied. "I think it would be acceptable. We can find you stockings to hang before Christmas here in this house. Then when you go to Granny's on Christmas Day, you'll have a stocking there to celebrate with them, too."

"Problem solved. And I think it's time a little girl gets ready for bed. Run tell your grandparents good night."

Charlie did as she was told.

"I'm surprised she didn't try to weasel more time out of me tonight."

"I saw a couple of yawns escape her when she thought no

one was looking. It's been a long day for her. But now that the angel is in place and all is well, I think she was glad to be told to go to bed." Emma began stacking empty boxes and picking up pieces of tinsel from the floor. Cole took the boxes out of her hands and set them to the side.

"It's been long for you, too. I'll put these things in the attic. You went out of your way to make this a special evening for everyone and you've earned a chance to relax. Mom and dad are leaving so how about we share some of the dessert and enjoy the fire in here in peace and quiet?"

Emma couldn't think of anything lovelier. But, then again, that would be pushing the limits of her self-control and blurring the lines again in her heart. Being alone with Cole would only open the wounds that needed to stay closed. There was no future for her there in that house.

Cole was going to do whatever needed to be done to keep Charlie happy and to appease Pamela. And if there was any credence in the woman's comments from the previous days, then a reconciliation and forgiveness might be a very real solution for all involved. And that was the last place she needed to be… in the middle of that possibility. Sitting in a room with Christmas songs playing and a warm fire inviting a cozy snuggle in front of it, was something for a couple with the future before them. None of this was for her.

"It's late and I'm more tired than I realized. I'll leave you to enjoy the peace and a slice of pie all to yourself. Goodnight."

She was glad Cole didn't try to talk her into staying. He just stood and watched her go. She was grateful. *Wasn't she?* Then why did her heart feel so awful?

THE NEXT MORNING, Emma was awake before the sun rose. She couldn't sleep so she finally got up and decided to go downstairs to start the coffee pot. Something caught her eye as she passed the doorway into the living room. The lights twinkled on the tree and she saw Charlie sitting in front of the tree, one arm around Angel who sat still as a statue beside her. Charlie was intent on the angel at the top of the tree. *What was it about that angel?*

Emma moved quietly into the room. She settled down next to the child.

"It's a beautiful tree, Charlie. And you picked the perfect angel for it."

The child nodded and smiled, her eyes still at the top of the tree.

"What is so special about the angel to you, Charlie? I'd really like to know. Unless it's some secret or something."

"It's not a secret," the child whispered. "Granny told me that if you have an angel on top of the tree, and you make a wish to her every night until Christmas, then that morning, your wish will come true... if you've been good and not forgotten to make your wish every night."

So that was it. She supposed that made sense to a child's believing mind. It had to be a very important wish.

"Can you tell me about the wish? Or is that not allowed?"

Charlie thought for a moment. Her voice lowered but there such a glow in her beautiful eyes as she shared with Emma. "I found my mother. I want the angel to make her want to be my mother. Then Christmas will be perfect."

The words were simple, but they shot to Emma's core. Had Charlie been able to find out about Pamela? She had just met her one time, correct? Could a child, even one abandoned so young, recognize her mother after so long? How else could one explain it? Charlie's heartfelt wish was for Pamela to be her mother. In that second, everything became crystal clear for Emma. In that second, everything had changed.

"I'M GLAD WE ran into each other. I did want to apologize again for any inconvenience I might have caused by showing up unannounced the other evening." Emma was caught off guard as Pamela appeared in the diner and slid into the booth across from her, uninvited. Emma had stopped into the diner to ask a favor of Darcy but she was busy with a delivery, so she waited.

Emma was struck again at how she could see the superficial beauty that had attracted both Drayton brothers to Pamela. And she was equally certain this woman was well-versed in using every ounce of her sexuality in getting whatever she wanted from a man. Cole had been lucky to escape her once. But he seemed to have some lapse of memory in recent days with her reappearance. Underneath the makeup and hair and the designer clothing, Emma sensed there wasn't much substance... and there certainly wasn't any signs of a heart.

"What is it you want?"

The woman's gaze narrowed and Emma was struck at how unattractive she really was when the façade cracked. "You do like to be direct, don't you? I can see that Mae might like that about you. But I don't think Cole would find that attractive. But be that as it may, I'm sure my attorneys can still make a jury believe all sorts of things about you."

Was she threatening Emma? Emma began to see red. *Keep it cool. Don't give her ammo.* She took a sip of her tea and counted to twenty. "You obviously have some threat you want to deliver so how about you stop wasting my time and yours and get to it?"

"You know, in some ways, you remind me of myself. I think we both know what we want when we see it. And you played your cards well. Getting Mae to invite you into their lives. Being the perfect little nanny for Charlie. Being there to comfort Cole. The problem about all of that... when the people of this little town start hearing certain things... well their regard for their clean sheriff and upstanding family might begin to crack."

"What is it you think you can do?"

"Throw enough mud at the wall and something will begin to stick. What do they seriously think has been going on in the sheriff's home, next door to his daughter's bedroom? Do they seriously think you two stay in your separate beds? What sort of fit father would put his child in such a situation? Need I say more about what my attorneys will do if Cole doesn't fall in line? Get lost now, and you'll be doing everyone a favor… Charlie most of all."

"That's rich that *now* you're thinking about the child you abandoned. How you live with yourself over that one, is something I can't understand. You don't care for her now and you don't care for Cole either. So, it must be money. The other brother drop you? He's smarter than I give him credit for if that's the case.

"And if your lawyers were so smart, they would have told you to keep your mouth shut… especially since there are so many listening devices around these days." With perfect timing, Emma brought her hand up… the cell phone visible in it. She smiled. She didn't need to say anything else. Pamela shot her a look that told her exactly what she could do with that phone and stormed out of the diner with a haughty toss of the bleached blonde hair. *Exit needs a bit more work, sweetie.*

"I was debating if I needed to come over here and toss

her out on her plastic keister or not. But looks like you handled it just fine on your own." Darcy walked up as Emma dropped the phone into the tote beside her. "Dare I ask the topic of conversation?"

"Just a friendly attempt at blackmail," Emma responded. She hoped she sounded more at ease than she felt. The anger was still boiling inside her. "I think we came to an agreement."

Darcy grinned. "I knew I liked you from the beginning."

"That's why I stopped by today... to ask a favor. I believe I can trust you with something important to me."

Darcy slid into the booth across from her. "I have a feeling I might not like this favor. But I'm ready to listen."

Emma had a feeling Darcy would hate the favor she was about to ask of her. But who else could she trust with something that meant so much?

"*Gone?* Gone where? Into Austin?" Cole looked at the woman who had barged into his office and caused him to disengage from a phone call with the county attorney.

The look on her face had told him before she spoke that something had gone terribly wrong someplace. Mae Drayton usually handled most issues with reason and calm. Her eyes were anything but calm. When she had announced herself by sailing through the doorway and then said, "She's gone.

Emma—"

He had no recourse but to question.

"No... she's really *gone*. As in *for good*. She left notes. Darcy just delivered mine. She said there was one for you that Emma left at your house. Did you have any idea about this?"

Cole felt as if he had been hit in the gut with a baseball bat. This news came out of the blue and just as lightning quick as a fast ball. He tried to marshal his thoughts that had scattered with the word *gone*. Emma couldn't be *gone*. There had to be some mistake.

He rose from his chair. "What did she say in your note?"

"She began by apologizing for having to ask me to pick up Charlie from school this afternoon. And she was sorry that she wouldn't be able to fulfill her bargain to stay until spring. But she had an opportunity for a job in the city and she needed to take it."

"And what did Darcy say? Anything?"

"Not much. But after a bit of coercing, I did get the fact from her that Pamela had words with Emma at the diner yesterday." She went on to tell Cole all she knew about what Darcy had described.

Cole anger rose. He had kept himself from strangling his ex-wife one too many times since her arrival. Now she had hurt Emma. *Emma*. Where had she gone?

He reached for his hat as he headed for the door, Mae close behind him. "What are you going to do?"

"I'm going home and read this note you said she left there. Then maybe I'll have a better handle on things. Tell Dad we need to meet with Paul as soon as we can. And if you can keep Charlie with you for a couple of days or until I can get on top of all this, it'd be a big help."

"Charlie—" his mother began and he stopped to look at her. "What, if anything, should we say to Charlie about all of this?"

"Nothing right now. As far as she needs to know... Emma had an emergency and had to go take care of some family business or something. Make something believable up... something that will buy us some time."

"This is one of those times when I hate lying to a child but it's our only recourse. The truth would hurt her too much right now."

"We don't know what the truth is right now, Mother. Let me do some investigating. I'll be in touch."

He turned but Mae's hand on his arm stopped him. He glanced down at her. "Find her, son. I just need to know she's okay." There was a shimmer in her eyes and his gut twisted even more. He knew exactly how she felt.

HIS NOTE WAS propped on the dining room table. It wasn't much more than Mae's.

I'm sorry I couldn't give you more notice, but this career opportunity came and I could not pass it up. We're just two months shy of my planned departure. But plans have a way of changing. With Charlie's mother being back and all the issues that need to be addressed with that, and finding what was for the good of all concerned, I believed it was the best decision to remove myself and allow the family the freedom needed to consider the future without a stranger in your midst.

I will miss each of you more than I can say and will cherish all the memories I take with me. Please give Charlie my love and let her know that I'm praying she gets her heart's wish and I know the angel on the tree will provide it. As for Angel, the dog… I know you were not fond of her in the beginning, but I think she's been accepted as one of your family now. It would be wrong of me to take her away from Charlie. If you find she is a nuisance, Darcy has assured me she will be glad to find her a good home. Just let her know.

Goodbyes are not my favorite thing. And this one is most difficult. Please know that I will never forget any moment of my time with your family.

Emma'

THAT'S IT? HE sat stunned after the first reading. It didn't improve much no matter how many times he went over it…

word by word. What had he done wrong? Had he pushed his feelings on her too fast? Maybe not fast enough? Too much? Too little? Expected something that was never there? Had he misread her responses? He could have sworn she felt the same things he did. He had taken another chance on trusting a woman with his heart... because this one was different. Was she? Or was she just like Pamela? Cut and run when something better came along? He could have sworn his life on the fact Emma was different. But she had left. That was the bottom line. What right did he have to think she would want to come back if he could find her? There were too many questions and he had no idea where to find the right answers.

Chapter Sixteen

THE ADULTS SAT around the table in the Draytons' kitchen. They had talked and talked the subject out until they were exhausted. Emma had been gone for almost a week.

"I agree with Cole," Vernon said, rubbing a large hand over his face and considering the emptiness of his coffee mug. "It's time to tell Charlie. She's going to be more upset the longer we wait. She has to know that Emma is not coming back as much as we might hope otherwise."

"I'm not ready to throw in the towel and say that's that." Mae was a definite holdout in the group.

Cole sat quietly, his gaze watching the faint snowflakes fall outside the kitchen window. The first snow of the season… possibly the only one. Christmas was still a week away. He didn't think he had the heart to draw out Charlie's heartbreak until after the holidays. Her birthday was two weeks after Christmas, so, either way, one important event was going to be ruined for the child.

A knock sounded at the backdoor and then Darcy's familiar voice was heard. Mae rose to greet her and get her coat hung up. Cole poured her a cup of coffee as she joined them at the table. She warmed her hands around the sides of the mug.

"I didn't realize it would start snowing when I called for you to come join us." Mae apologized.

"Nonsense. It's not sticking on the road. I enjoy being out in the country. Do I need to ask what this is about or can I just guess by the long faces, sleepless eyes, and absence of the usual Drayton smiles? We are discussing Emma?"

"We're trying to put some sense to it and decide on telling Charlie now before Christmas or afterwards and before her birthday. Neither is an easy decision. I suppose we were just hoping that there was something you might share. Anything you gleaned—" Mae was interrupted by her son.

"Mother, face it. Emma was upfront with us from the beginning. You came across her that day and she told you her plans… her dreams. She wouldn't have been in McKenna Springs at all if she hadn't had car issues. This was never more for her than a stopgap to get her on the road again. You want to hold on to some fairy tale you have in your mind."

"Yes, I admit it," Mae spoke up. "I want a happy ending for us all. And for Emma. I had the distinct impression that meant she wanted to stay right here, with us… with Charlie and with you. Then something happened."

Cole gave a deep sigh. He looked at Darcy who was looking at the floor beside her. "Okay, Darcy. I will ask what your opinion is. Is there anything else you can add that we haven't talked about already this week?"

Darcy took a moment and looked at each face around the table. "I made a promise to Emma. But sometimes promises can't always be kept when weighted against the greater good of a situation. What would I want done if the shoe was on the other foot?"

"These are things I know. I know that Emma loved being with Charlie. She loved being part of your lives and the life of McKenna Springs. She just seemed to really want to be part of everything and I think she saw that she could find herself staying right here."

Vernon asked the question that hung in the air. "But? What's the 'but' in all of that?"

"But that seemed to change when Pamela showed up. I could sense her stepping back. I know that there was something Pamela told her when she came to the house that night. That planted a seed of doubt in Emma's mind. Then she mentioned what Charlie had said to her, about this wish Charlie had, and I think that made her decision. She needed to leave and not give anyone any cause to hesitate because of her. That's what I know."

"So, you're saying she left because of Pamela? And what does Charlie have to do with anything? Whatever could that child have said?" Mae glanced toward the den where Charlie and Angel were watching movies.

"It's time we find out. We can ask Charlie, but what can

we do about Pamela? She's gone for good, but Emma doesn't know that." Vernon added.

"I think Pamela gave Emma the distinct impression that you and she were getting back together." Darcy leveled a solemn gaze on Cole.

"Whatever made her think that?" Cole was shocked.

"Well, being a woman, and thinking what a woman like Pamela is capable of, I would say it had something to do with sex."

"Mother!" Cole couldn't believe the words coming out of her mouth.

Vernon shook his head. "We're all adults here, son. I agree with your mom. Think about it. How was Emma acting before that evening toward you? Then afterwards? If I wanted to get rid of someone I considered a rival in some way... well, we've seen how low Pamela has stooped in the past."

Cole thought back over the days and nights, the conversations... and things had changed just about that time. He had chalked it up to Emma having been so concerned and worried from the surprise visit after the incident in the tree lot with Charlie. Why had he just *assumed*? Then he remembered the bit Emma had spoken about gloves the night Pamela came to the house. How could he have let that go?

And he had drawn back a bit from pushing time with Emma and having that talk they never got around to having... had she construed that as his withdrawing from her?

Changing his mind? Wanting to get back with the mother of his child? A light was dawning big time.

Cole stood and went into the den. He lowered himself to sit beside his daughter, Indian-style on the carpet. "How's the movie going?"

She gave the shoulder-shrug. She had grown quieter of late. He had assumed it was because of Emma. *Stop assuming.* "You don't seem as excited as you were about Christmas. What happened?"

"What if Emma doesn't get back before Christmas? She needs to be here."

The words were rough to hear. They echoed his thoughts almost every moment of the day since Emma had left. Only he wanted her for a lot longer than just this Christmas. He had a hunch Charlie did, too.

"Did you and Emma have a talk about the angel on top of the tree before she had to leave to take care of her business?"

Charlie looked up at him. She seemed to be deciding something in her mind before she responded to the question. She nodded.

"Can you tell me about that?"

"I told her about why I make a wish every night with the angel on the tree."

"And can you share that with me?"

"I told her about how Granny said that my wishes would come true if there was an angel on my tree and I wished really hard. On Christmas morning, the angel would make my wish come true. My wish where I get the mommy I really want. But if Emma's not here, I won't get the one I want. I didn't tell her, but she's the mommy I asked the angel to bring."

Everything made sense. Cole shook his head. "Thank you, sweetheart." He dropped a kiss on his daughter's head before he stood up.

"Do you think the angel will bring Emma back in time?"

Cole hoped the angel was listening… that angels everywhere were listening to his words. "I think the angel will do all she can to make that happen."

Cole strode through the kitchen to the wall phone. The three people still seated at the kitchen table watched in mystified silence. "Davis, I need another favor. I need to take you up on that offer of that tracker you spoke about. I need to reach him tonight. There's not much time to waste."

"THAT SNOW IS really coming down, but it should let up in another few hours according to the weather report." One of the truckers shared that bit of news as he slid into one of the vacant seats at the counter of the café. He smiled as Emma set the cup of coffee in front of him.

"Walt's really improved the scenery around here. Sure you don't want to have me show you around town? I know all the fun places."

"I'm sure. I don't have time to socialize. Too busy looking for a job in the city." She set the coffeepot back on the burner on the counter. The burger plate was in the window and she took it and the ticket to the man seated at the opposite end of the bar. The snow had caused it to be an early night for most of the traffic they usually had at that hour. Emma minded simply because it meant she had more time on her hands. Time thoughts could intrude upon.

She didn't need that to happen. She didn't want to think about what a certain little girl was doing at the moment or what her daddy was doing either. Those thoughts weren't helping anything. She had hoped with each day that passed, she would think less of what she left behind in McKenna Springs. She had travelled almost three hundred miles north. It wouldn't matter if it had been three thousand. The distance would never lessen the pain in her heart. She had to learn to live with it. And slowly, things would get better. They had to.

Tomorrow would be her day off. She had three more places in mind to place applications. One bank in Fort Worth had offered her an interview at the end of the week. She had to hope that might be the one that would get her out of the roadside café on the outskirts of the city and onto the road to using her education. In the meantime, her skills at serving food came in handy to pay for the efficiency apartment that was in walking distance of the café. That certainly saved on gas and wear and tear on her pickup. Her savings wouldn't last all that long so she had to be frugal.

Christmas songs were playing from the speakers in the ceiling. She would be so glad when the season was gone. Every tree, every angel, every song... all were reminders of those people she had come to love... and then lost. So much for the holiday spirit and believing in miracles.

The door chime signaled another customer needed her attention. She automatically reached for the coffee pot and a mug. She turned to the person who had taken a seat behind her. Thankfully, her grip held on the pot of coffee. Cole Drayton's gaze was locked on hers. It was just as mesmerizing as she remembered and just as piercing. He wasn't smiling. He was dressed in his uniform with a heavy leather jacket with a sheepskin collar turned up against the cold of the evening. A few flakes of snow melted on the dark brown crown of his hat. The badge and gun had drawn the attention of his fellow diners. They averted their eyes onto their own business.

"Coffee?"

"Please." He wasn't lowering his gaze.

She had to concentrate hard to keep from spilling the hot liquid. Her hand wanted to shake but she was determined to keep it steady. She set the pot on the burner and then turned back.

"Would you like a menu?"

"No thanks. Just a cup of coffee." Cole raised the mug to

his lips and took a couple of sips. He had no problem with shaky hands.

He seemed quite relaxed as he settled in to the spot at the counter. *If he would just stop with the staring.* The man beside him engaged him in a couple of questions and he responded. All just friendly conversation. She moved down the counter, trying to keep her mind on finishing her duties as her shift was over in less than a half hour. She could scoot out the back and he wouldn't even know. That was the plan. If she could just get her breathing to calm down and her pulses to stop hammering in her ears.

To her surprise, she saw him rise, lay a bill on the counter, and without a glance in her direction, he left the café and went out into the night. He left. *Just like that.* What had made him appear if only to leave without more than a half dozen words to her? Maybe he just wanted to what? Gloat? Make certain she wasn't anywhere close to his perfect life? Why had he felt the need to just show up? And then he left. *Guess he got his fill of slumming.* Emma didn't know why she should be so angry and hurt both at the same time. He was gone. *Good.* Now put it behind her. She'd be moving on herself in a few weeks or less. *Why did he have to come at all?*

She pushed him to the back of her mind while she finished up her evening shift. Bundled up in coat and scarf over her head and secured around her neck, she pulled on her gloves and headed out into the darkness for the walk to her apartment. Christmas lights shone along the way. The small town had some pretty decorations from lantern stands lining the sidewalk and somewhere there was music being piped in along the way. More Christmas music. And when White Christmas began to play, the snowflakes took it as their cue to grow larger. Any other time, she would have found the moment to be perfect. Any other year that would be... but not this one.

A tall form materialized in front of her and she halted in surprise. She hadn't expected to see Cole standing in front of her. She had thought he had left a while ago. Evidently, he had something on his mind.

"You should be careful walking alone at this hour."

The lawman speaks. "I am aware of the dangers of walking alone. I don't have far to go. And I have mace in my hand in my pocket."

Was that a hint of smile? *Don't smile.* She couldn't stay strong if he turned on that smile. "Thanks for the heads-up. I won't make any sudden moves."

"Why are you here and how did you find me in the first place? This is way out of your jurisdiction and don't try to tell me you were in the neighborhood." Might as well get the cards out on the table.

He evidently had something he needed to get off his chest. "It might be warmer if we talk at your place."

"And I'm fine right here. I don't think we have much to talk about."

He glanced around and made a decision. "There's a gazebo at the end of the block. Let's go sit for a minute." He didn't wait for an agreement and his hand was at her elbow.

She could make a scene but to what end? He could be stubborn as a mule when he put his mind to it. She went along with the plan. The gazebo had benches around the railings. Lights twinkled off and on over its roof and around each pillar. Now and then passersby would happen along the sidewalks but, for the most part, they were alone on the snowy night. He waited until she was seated and then he took his place, much too close to hers. It made it more difficult to concentrate.

"Okay. I found you because a very good tracker was able to trace your path in one of the many ways he has to make my job a lot easier."

"I wasn't trying to hide. I left notes explaining why and what I was doing."

"Yes, you did. But not exactly *why*. I think that's what needs some clarification. It took a while but, you see, there are some people back in McKenna Springs that happen to care a hell of a lot about you, and have been pretty miserable since you left, and they just won't give up. *Not yet*. Not until we have the *truth*."

"Is Charlie okay?" She hated the vision that came to her of the little girl upset.

"No. She isn't. She mopes around the house, or drives me crazy with 'remember how Emma used to make the pancakes in funny shapes? Could you try to tie the bow like

Emma can? Emma said this or Emma said that'... you are a lot to live up to."

"Sorry that I'm such a thorn in your happy side. But she'll get over things... kids are tough. Besides with Christmas coming soon, she'll have a lot of other things to concentrate on."

"I don't think you're sorry at all... at least not about being a thorn in my side. And kids aren't all that tough all the time. I know some adults who sure aren't strong. Mae and Vernon to name a couple. Darcy for another one. People stop me every day, wanting to know where you are and when you'll be back. Not that you give them much thought probably."

"Are you trying to make me angry? Because I don't see the point in you coming all this way at all. My stay in McKenna Springs was never to be permanent. You said that more than a few times yourself."

"So, I did." He gave a sigh and his gaze looked up to the sky.

A few snowflakes blew around them on the night breeze and one ended up on his lashes. Emma had to resist the urge to brush it away. She kept her hands curled inside her pockets. He dropped his silver gaze back on her. It wasn't as cold as it was before. She certainly didn't need to see any of those remembered looks he could give her that made her knees go weak and threaten to melt her into butter with their heat.

"I guess people just got confused. They had hoped you might have changed your mind and wanted to stay longer."

"Things change. People change. It was best I kept to the plan."

"Waitressing in a small café in an out of the way town, is that part of the plan?"

"I have interviews at the end of the week. I won't be here for long."

Cole's eyes darkened. He seemed to have the need to move. He stood; his hands came out of his pockets to rest just above the gun belt at the sides of his waist. Was he going into his lawman mode of interrogating? She had her answer soon enough.

"Did you leave because of Pamela? Something she said to you… something she might have mentioned about her and me or her delusions along that score?"

Emma hesitated. What was the best course to take? He didn't give her long to think.

"The truth, Emma. Direct questions require direct answers."

"Yes. Once she told me how *close* the two of you had become since she had returned, it was clear I needed to not be any sort of obstacle to your reuniting and making a family for Charlie."

He blew out a frustrated sigh. "I see. So Pamela gave you the impression that she and I had reunited and you believed her? What about how close I thought *you* and *I* were on the way to becoming? Or was that just a figment of my imagination?"

"No. But that was *before* she came back. Things changed then. I didn't want you to think there was any reason you had to give me... us... *our* situation a second thought." She was stumbling with her thoughts.

"You took whatever she told you at face value. Without giving me the benefit of the doubt."

"Where is Pamela? Still in McKenna Springs?"

"It took some negotiations... a little bit of blackmail... and some interesting court documents from her time in California. In the end, cold cash saved the day. Pamela left the country a rich lady. She signed documents and she can never come into Charlie's life again. She found that life in South America or some such place might be more to her liking. It took a while for all that to happen because I knew two things as a lawman. As much as one might wish to place their total faith in the judicial system, things can go wrong and not all judges should be administering the laws at all. I had seen too many cases where there was a clear-cut case to remove a child from a mother but, no matter what, the judge ended up siding with the mother... no matter how bad she might have been.

"That was a role of the dice I wasn't prepared to take. I knew if I had the time and dug deep enough and long enough, there would be something that would make it impossible for any court to allow her back into Charlie's life.

I called her bluff and it helped she admitted she could be bought off for the right amount of cash. And that was overheard by a pair of rangers who were listening. That was what took time and why I might not have been able to cover all the bases I wanted to, but I had one thought and that was Charlie. I needed to make certain that Pamela could never be a threat to my family ever again. I had to hope you would understand that."

"It would have been easier if I had known some of this at the time. But I just knew I had to do whatever I could to make things easier… for everyone concerned. I'm glad that Charlie is safe from her."

"Pamela was one part of the problem. That's been dealt with. Now, did Charlie say something to you about the angel and a wish before you left?"

His swift change of questioning caught her off guard. "Yes."

"What did she say?"

"She wanted her mother back. That's what she wants more than anything for Christmas. I believed that somehow, she knew who Pamela was. If that was the case, I knew it was time to get out of the way and let your family do what it needed to do to heal itself. So, I left. End of story."

"You don't know the full story. Charlie wanted the angel to bring her the mother *she* wants for Christmas. You *assumed* she meant Pamela. How could she want that when she has never met the woman nor seen a photo of her or even knows of her existence?" He drew within a foot of her and his hands reached out. She placed hers in them automatically and he drew her to stand in front of him. Emma had to look up a bit to see his face that was half in shadows.

"The mother Charlie has begged that angel for each and every night is not and never was Pamela."

"Then who? I don't—"

"*You.* Charlie wants *you.* In her mind, the angel was the one sure way she had of making her dream come true. Mae and Vernon want you. Half of, if not all, the town wants *you.* Does that make any difference at all?" His voice changed and a tone came into it... the one that made her bones all quivery was there.

Emma realized just how much she had missed hearing it. His hands found their way to her shoulders. Her breathing was having some difficulty.

"Does it make any difference when I say that I knew you'd be trouble from the moment I found you in my bed that night when Mae brought you home? It was sealed as fact that next morning when I hauled you out of that engine and you stood there with that scraggly mutt beside you... your blue eyes not giving an inch. I just didn't realize what kind of trouble you might be until later.

"As the days passed and I found myself getting used to beginning the day with your smile and hearing laughter from you and Charlie in the next room, or watching how you engaged people and had them your best friends in nothing flat... your efforts to bring life to the garden around the house, planting your bulbs to bloom in the spring... wanting to make it beautiful for all of us. There are so many things.

"You became something *more* before I knew it. And it wasn't trouble you brought. You brought a second chance to live life with a love I never knew could exist because I never had found it before you. But then Pamela arrived. I felt you slipping away, but I was too involved in trying to fight the danger that she brought with her to also see that something far more important was slipping away at the same time. And then you were gone. It hurt. It made me question if I had misread how you felt. Maybe I had trusted in the wrong person again. I thought that's what you wanted... to leave.

"And it took a group of friends and family, one silly dog, and one feisty, maddening, beautiful woman to make me a believer. I added my own wish to the angel on top of the tree at home... right before I left to come here. I'm believing in a Christmas angel to not let me down."

"A tough lawman like yourself?"

His smile was so endearing and so perfect and it lit the night with warmth. "This tough lawman has the same Christmas wish as his daughter and everyone else in McKenna Springs who loves you. Come home, Emma. I love you and that's my Christmas wish for now and always. Be my wife and be the mother Charlie has chosen for herself. Will you be our Christmas wish come true?"

The moisture in her eyes was the visible happiness erupting in her heart. Cole had said the magic word... *love.* He wanted her for a lifetime, not just a few months. Everything she had ever dreamed about in her young years had come to stand in front of her in that moment. Cole offered her a home... filled with love and laughter and beauty and the promise that she would never be alone again. It had indeed become her turn and all things possible had become her reality.

Emma's palms lifted to hold his dear face between them. His love shone like a beacon down upon her. Cole was her destiny, her world... her dream come true.

The answer was the easiest one she'd ever make. "I think that angel has worked overtime... bringing us all together in one place, at the right time, and opening our hearts to the greatest gift of all this Christmas. I love you. I love Charlie. And I want to sit in a rocker on that front porch beside you each and every night for the rest of my life."

Cole's kiss would be her treasured memory of a Christmas that had brought the best miracle of all to hearts that believed in a child's simplest faith in a wish. They kissed beneath the twinkling lights and shimmering snowflakes... two hearts beating as one.

Christmas, McKenna Springs, Texas...

CHRISTMAS MORNING FOUND a fresh mantel of snow covering the ground around the ranch house. It glistened like a blanket of diamonds in the early morning sunrise. All was quiet inside. Then, the silence was broken by a creak on the staircase. A couple of moments later, Charlie, clad in her purple and pink nightgown and slippers, appeared in the doorway to the living room. Angel trailed her.

The solemn-faced child approached the tree and looked at the angel still smiling down at her from the top of the tree. Nothing had changed. The brightly-wrapped presents under the tree's branches did not claim her attention. The stockings stuffed with goodies weren't noticed. Charlie slowly shook her head and sank to the floor, Angel nudging her arm until it could snuggle closer to the child in dual commiseration.

"It didn't work Angel. The angel on the tree didn't listen. She didn't make my wish come true."

"Are you so sure about that?"

Both Charlie and the dog jerked their heads around at the voice coming from the woman standing in the doorway. Emma moved forward and Charlie sat speechless. She took no note of Cole and his parents moving to stand in the hallway, watching the scene unfold.

"It's Christmas morning. You asked the angel for the mother you chose. I believe the angel said that was me. Was she right? Is your Christmas wish that you want *me* to be your mother?"

Charlie was on her feet. Her nod was emphatic. "Yes, you're the one! I really, really want you more than anything. I promise I'll be a really good daughter and I'll always try to remember my manners and I'll—"

Emma knelt in front of the child and gathered her small hands inside hers. "Charlie, you don't have to promise me all of that. It's enough that you love me as much as I love you... and as much as I love your daddy and granny and grampy...and even Angel. I would be very proud to be your mother for the rest of my life. Merry Christmas, my sweet little angel girl."

Charlie's reply was to wrap her arms around Emma's neck in a tight hug that Emma knew she would always remember because it meant she had found that place she had always sought... that place where the Christmas spirit lived all year long in the hearts of those who believe in the magic of miracles and wishes made to angels... no matter what shape or form they might take. Cole joined them and drew them both into the wide circle of his arms. *They were home.* And the angel on top of the tree shone brighter than ever upon them.

Epilogue

"SEVEN DAYS. ONE week. Either way you say it, it doesn't get any longer or give us any more time to plan and prepare for a wedding." Mae Drayton shook her head, hands on hips, brow furrowed in deep consideration.

The Christmas gifts had been opened, stockings emptied, and the Christmas dinner would soon be on the dining table at Mae and Vernon's home. Charlie and Angel were in the den watching the movie Santa had placed in her stocking. Every few minutes she would take time out and run into the kitchen, giving quick hugs to her dad and especially to Emma. Her smiles couldn't get any wider as she danced around the room and then ran back to watch more of the animated movie.

"Well, you've always been one to work miracles, Mother. I'm sure this will be no different." Cole grinned across the kitchen at her, slowly rising from his chair at the table in the alcove where he and his dad had been told to sit and stay out of the way... advice they were pleased to follow. With coffee mug in hand, Cole moved to lean against the kitchen cabinet, close to where Emma was busy placing the homemade yeast rolls onto the baking pan.

"And maybe Emma has other ideas. She might not want to be so rushed down the aisle. A perfect wedding takes some time." Mae sought confirmation from her future daughter-in-law.

Emma patted her hands on the front of the apron she wore and turned her attention to the matter at hand. "I think seven days might be an issue."

Mae nodded an I-told-you-so toward her son. That did not last long as Emma's next words followed with a saucy grin.

"Seven days is a bit long. I told Cole I was fine with a justice of peace tomorrow morning at the court house."

"A justice of peace? Oh, my Lord... Vernon don't just sit there with a silly grin on your face... help me talk some sense into these two." Mae's gaze moved back to Emma. "Wedding days are special and there are so many people who want to help celebrate such a day. Surely, you'd like a cake and flowers and—" She stopped when she caught the look Emma and Cole shared, both having problems keeping their laughter contained. "You two ought to be ashamed of yourselves. You've been pulling my leg!"

"I'm sorry, Mae," Emma replied. "These two men talked me into this joke."

"It is only partly a joke," Cole amended. "I am serious about seven days. We plan to be married next Saturday night so we can celebrate the New Year as the beginning of our life together."

"We need to get busy. First, we need to call the pastor and see about the church and—" Mae stopped when she saw the tentative look on Emma's face. "No church?"

"I would really like to have the wedding at Cole's home."

"*Our* home," he corrected, the look he gave Emma warmed her all the way to the tips of her toes. "That's what will happen then. I chose the day, and the rest is however Emma wants it to be. I think I can trust you, Mom, to see it's everything my bride deserves." His hand covered one of Emma's and she returned the squeeze he gave hers. It was still incredible, the feeling that filled her whenever she met his gaze and saw the immense amount of love that shown there. Love for *her*.

"It will be a day to remember all your lives. I guarantee that."

"And now that is settled, can we get that turkey carved anytime soon?" Vernon chimed in and brought them back to the matter at hand.

The dining table was beautiful with its cream linens and silver-rimmed china. A large centerpiece of poinsettias and holly surrounded two hurricane candles. The turkey was perfectly browned and there was an assortment of bowls filled with dressing, vegetables, fruit salads… more than enough for a celebration. As they joined hands for the blessing delivered by Vernon, Emma's heart felt as if it would burst. Suddenly, she had so much to be thankful for, so much had changed in her life in such a short time. She had never dared to think that one day she would have the love of a good man like Cole Drayton, or be the mother of a beautiful little girl like Charlie. And she had found a family in Mae and Vernon and all the caring friends in McKenna Springs. The angel had more than blessed their Christmas.

The food was delicious. Most of the talk centered on wedding planning and Charlie couldn't help but chime in with her request.

"Can I have a new dress… a party dress and can it be purple?"

"That's up to Emma, the bride, to choose what colors to have at her wedding," Mae replied.

Emma smiled at the child's enthusiasm. "I think there is every possibility we'll find a beautiful dress just for you. And purple is definitely in the color scheme." She finished with a wink at the little girl.

It seemed that the clock jumped into high gear after that dinner. Time sped at a faster rate. They did find a perfect outfit for Charlie. Black suits with western piping at the yokes with black boots and hats were easily chosen for Cole and Vernon and the same for Davis, who agreed to be Cole's best man. Vernon had been given a special duty for the wedding. The evening after the Christmas dinner had been put away and people were enjoying the firelight and soft talk in the living room, Emma had drawn Vernon outside on the porch.

"So, what secret are we sharing out here?" He had grinned at her.

Emma took a deep breath. The butterflies were suddenly racing around inside her stomach. She hoped the man would agree with the request she was about to make of him. "I don't have any family as you know... I was going to just walk down the aisle on my own. But I... well, I was thinking that maybe I could ask if you might... and it's okay if you don't agree and don't..."

"If you're trying to ask me if I would give you my arm down that aisle on the grandest day in our lives in a long, long while, then you don't need to say anything else." Was that a hint of moisture in his gray eyes that filled with warmth and his ever-present smile? A sudden knot of emotion had formed in Emma's throat as she saw and heard his response. "It would be the greatest of honors for me. I never had a daughter so I thought that privilege would never come my way. But I couldn't have chosen a better wife for my son and a better mother for Charlie. And I have come to think of you as more a daughter, than a daughter-in-law. You make this old man very happy."

She had been drawn into a tight bear hug at that point and laughter had freed the butterflies.

"YOU'RE CERTAIN THIS is what you want? To get married *here*, in the sun room in front of the fireplace?" Cole sounded a bit skeptical, but Emma didn't blame him. He had gone along with everything so far without question. If she was pleased, that was good enough for him he had said.

"It will look different on Saturday. Just use your imagination. With flowers and plants and candles arranged just right, and we can open the double doors into the living room and if the weather cooperates, the doors leading out onto the porch can be opened back and there will be plenty of room for the eighty guests that have been invited to the ceremony."

"And the rest of the guests will get invites to the reception and dance at Mom and Dad's place and we will all ring in the New Year at midnight. Then you and I will make our getaway. Unless you decide to take me up on my standing offer to take you away right now and we just elope and..." Cole's voice faded away and he grinned as he saw the look he was receiving from her. "I know... I was just kidding. Can't blame a bridegroom for trying."

She playfully squeezed the arm that she had her hands wrapped around as they stood on the porch of the house that would soon be her permanent home. "I just want us to say our vows in the house that we'll share for the rest of our lives. I knew the moment I laid eyes on this house, the day Mae brought me here, that I felt there was something special about it. It was a little forlorn here and there, but it just needed some love and care and it would be perfect. It holds so much of your family history... and this will be another chapter... *our* chapter."

Cole dropped a soft kiss on her forehead as she pressed

her head against his shoulder. "You brought it alive... and me, too. And I agree that our lives with Charlie... and any other children we might be blessed to have... should be celebrated as beginning right here."

Emma turned to go down the steps, but Cole's hands kept her beside him. Her gaze questioned him.

"When I proposed to you that night in Ft. Worth, I didn't bring a ring. In my haste to get to you, I overlooked that important element." He withdrew a small, blue velvet box from his jacket pocket.

Emma's pulses began to race. This was one of those moments that a girl would remember for the rest of her life. It was a moment she never dared to dream about.

"You love family history and all, so you'll appreciate this, I think. When my grandfather married my grandmother, they didn't have much to start their lives with. Just a small four-room house on sixty acres. They managed to buy two small bands of gold. Three years later, after their first really good crop of cotton came in, he bought her what he called a proper ring." He opened the box and Emma caught her breath.

The ring sparkled in the sunlight, but its unique design caught her imagination right away. It resembled a rose in bloom... the center of the rose was the largest of the diamonds. Smaller diamonds formed the petals and the band had diamonds in leaf patterns.

"I realize that you might not like the design, so we can

have it reset in any—"

"*No...* absolutely not," Emma spoke up right away. "This is so gorgeous just as it is. I love it."

"The ring began with the center stone. Then each year for the next forty-two years, another stone was added until the rose bloomed as you see it now. My granddad said Grandma was the most beautiful rose in the gardens around this house so he wanted a rose for her ring."

Cole took the ring from the box and reached for her hand. The ring slid on and they both shared a quiet moment as the jewels sparkled on its new mistress.

Emma's free hand made a quick swipe at the corner of one eye. "It's the most beautiful ring I've ever seen. I'll cherish it forever."

"And I will cherish *you* forever." Cole's lips claimed hers in a tender kiss that served to seal his words. "Now, while you do the measurements for Mae that she needed for the sunroom, I need to check the barn area and see about parking plans for those wedding guests. I'll meet you back here in a few minutes." They went their separate ways.

A little while later, with measurements on the paper in her pocket, Emma returned and sat on the porch steps to wait for him. Her eyes kept being drawn to the ring on her hand.

Cole approached her across the soft grass. There was something about the set of her shoulders that caught his attention. Was she upset about something? Where was the smile of a happy bride-to-be?

"Hey, I know I'm running us late to the party Darcy and Stacy are hosting, but I just needed to—"

"It's okay. We have time."

"No, it's not okay. You've been crying. What's wrong?"

She shook her head to toss it off. "It's just bridal jitters."

He wasn't buying the trite excuse. He glimpsed real pain in those eyes before she lowered her lashes and stood, preparing to head towards the truck.

"It's more than that. Talk to me, Emma." His hands gathered hers into them and stopped her retreat. He waited.

"I'm scared."

"Scared? Of what?"

"I'm scared that all of this will go away. It's like I'm dreaming and everything is so perfect and happy and what if I wake up and none of this... you, Charlie, Mae... all of it... what if it's not real? And you can think me silly or overreacting, and maybe I am, but that's why I'm crying."

He gathered her into his arms and he didn't laugh. His breath was warm against her forehead as his lips touched her. His hand meant to soothe away the fears from her mind as it smoothed over her hair in a repeated motion. "I'm not laughing, sweetheart. I know what you mean. I've felt the same way."

"You have?" Those glittering eyes raised to meet his. "Why?"

"I never expected to have such happiness, either. I was

content in my life... or so I thought until you came along. That's why I was such an arrogant fool in the beginning with you. You scared me. What I *felt* for you scared me, because I knew what pain there would be if and when you did leave. I pushed you away to avoid the pain. But then I realized that as long as I held your hand in mine, I wasn't scared. I could jump off any cliff as long as we were together. And I just needed to have faith in the fact that you did love me and we will get through anything... *together.* This *is* all real and I am not going anyplace... unless you're with me."

"Whither thou goest, I will go also," she murmured the ages-old words, the warmth of their love chasing away all the dark clouds of doubt. Her hand in his increased the strength they shared.

And those same words were the ones they repeated to each other in front of a multitude of family and friends when their day arrived. The house had been transformed with candlelight in hurricane lanterns throughout the rooms, huge baskets of red roses and white lilies and poinsettias adorned corners and steps and garland entwined staircases and mantels. Soft music chosen by the bride and groom was provided via a pianist. Guests greeted each other and mingled in the beautiful rooms as Vernon circulated and made certain all were made welcome.

Upstairs, Mae helped put the finishing touches on the bride's hair, which had been swept up and back in an elegant chignon. Fresh flowers adorned the clip at the back of her hair that held the soft, elbow-length veil of lace in place. The day they had gone through the trunks in the attic for clothing for Mae and Vernon's anniversary party, Emma had spotted a dress in a tissue-laden box and she had but one dress in mind when it came time to choose a wedding dress. None of the wedding dresses in the stores they shopped in Austin had removed it from her mind. She had told Mae what she really wanted… but she hadn't been sure her request would be granted. Mae had taken a few moments as she stood in the living room after hearing what Emma had asked.

"You really want to wear that dress? It needs some taking in at the seams and the design is outdated a bit and—"

"If you'd rather not, I understand. But I think it's too beautiful to just stay in a box in an attic. Of course, we might keep looking in the stores and…"

"No more looking. That dress was meant for you. And the fact you love it as I did when I wore it, makes it all the more special. And we'll make a few changes to make it even more beautiful and all yours."

The dress was her "something old" but looked as if it had stepped out of a bridal magazine page. The portrait collar with its deep white satin accentuated Emma's beauty. The rest of the dress with its fitted waist and flared, tea-length skirt was white lace over the same satin. Slim lace sleeves went to her wrists. Cole's wedding gift to her of a single strand of pearls with pearl and diamond earrings to match were perfect accessories.

"You look like Cinderella," Charlie said in a child's awe, standing beside the two women as they gazed in the mirror at their handiwork.

Emma smiled at her. "I think I feel like Cinderella today. It's perfect."

"But not complete," Mae said, reaching into a box on the small table beside her. Mae handed over a small, white leather-bound bible along with a cream lace-edged handkerchief to Emma. "I carried these under my bouquet when I married Vernon. My mother carried them before me. It's your turn now."

Moisture threatened and Emma had to blink to keep it at bay and keep from reapplying her makeup... again. Tears had already made it necessary once. "Thank you, Mae. For everything you've done for this day. For welcoming me into your family and for rescuing me that night in the diner when I was feeling pretty hopeless about life. You turned out to be a true guardian angel."

Mae looked at her with a soft smile lighting her eyes. "I think more than one angel was at work that night in our family. You came along when Charlie and I needed your help in the middle of nowhere. Cole's heart was reborn when you arrived in this house. I think guardian angels had their hands busy in all our lives in recent months."

"And my angel on the tree did the best job... she gave me the mother I wanted," Charlie chimed in. "And Angel is an angel too… if she hadn't got lost in the garage, then you wouldn't have rescued us at all. So, she has to be a real angel, too. Right?"

Both Emma and Mae grinned at the little girl and her simple statement.

Emma nodded her head. "Angels come in all forms when they're needed."

And Angel, the dog, wasn't done with her part. Several minutes later, the music changed and Darcy, in lavender satin, began the procession down the staircase and through the assembled guests. She was followed by Charlie, diligently doing her duty by dropping pale lavender rose petals along the cream runner. Her dress was floor-length and full-skirted in yards of white tulle with a bright purple satin sash tied in a bow at back. A matching bow was in her hair. The purple sparkles on her dress shoes showed now and then as she did her practiced step-glide-step.

The music changed and then it was Emma's turn. Vernon met her at the bottom of the staircase and she wasn't certain which of them would keep the tears at bay better. She carried a nosegay of lavender roses dotted with white freesia blossoms, along with the small bible and hanky.

When they turned and stepped into the sunroom, her heart went to her throat. She met Cole's steady gaze at that moment as he waited beside the pastor and Davis at the altar. The warmth in his eyes drew her on winged feet to his side. She remembered little else of the next few moments as they exchanged their vows. All the love she had searched for was shining upon her as he repeated his vows in a strong, steady voice, his gaze never wavering from hers.

And then came one more participant down the aisle. Charlie and Angel had worked each day on a special surprise. And Emma had forbidden anyone from discouraging Charlie's idea. On cue, Angel appeared on the aisle. As befitting a member of the wedding party, a ribbon and bow matching Charlie's purple satin, adorned the animal's neck. To one of the ends of the ribbon had been tied—by Vernon—the two gold bands. With tail wagging, ears flopping, and a happy grin, Angel trotted right up to the couple and sat down. Laughter and tears accompanied the sight which made the moment even more memorable. Cole retrieved the bands and gave a pat on the furry head for a job well done.

They were pronounced husband and wife. The kiss they shared went straight to Emma's core and drew her heart and soul to meet his in an eternal joining. Applause and more laughter next filled her reality. The celebration began in earnest as the group moved to the reception at Mae and Vernon's. One of his large barns had been transformed to an unbelievable fairyland of twinkling white lights, candles, and lively music from the dance band. When the lights dimmed and the music changed to a slow tune, Cole drew his bride to the dance floor. As the strains of their song began, Emma laid her head against his shoulder and closed her eyes. Never had she felt such utter bliss.

And, right on cue, at the end of the song, the countdown began. With Charlie gathered up in his arms and Emma's arm around both, they saw the New Year begin with more tears and smiles and much love of family and friends.

"Was today as wonderful as you wanted it to be? I know brides want the perfect day… or so I hear." Cole had carried her across the threshold a few minutes before and they were finally alone, having left Charlie with her grandparents.

He had left Emma for a moment to retrieve a heavier quilt from the couch. He asked the question as he returned to where she was sitting happily ensconced on the wedding present from Vernon and Mae. The day before the wedding, the gift had been delivered on the back of a truck bed from Miller Atkins Woodworks Shop in town. Miller delivered it himself. Emma couldn't contain her joy when she laid eyes on the intricately carved porch swing.

Cole took his place next to her and tucked the cover around them. She snuggled against his warmth, his arm drawing her in next to him.

"It was better than anything I could have ever hoped for. Everyone worked so hard to make it so special for us. It's a day I will never forget as long as I live. Thank you for all of it." She rose to place a kiss on his cheek.

He smiled down at her. "I think there are many more special days ahead for us. But the best part is we'll share them together. I take it that you're also pleased with this gift from Mom and Dad?"

"I love this swing. It's so beautiful."

"Well, Dad thought we needed to add it. He said rocking chairs were nice but a guy liked to snuggle with his girl and you couldn't do that in a rocker... not very comfortably at least." He grinned as he repeated the conversation.

"I think he's a very smart man. Snuggling does have its merits."

"I couldn't agree more. And I guess I shouldn't be surprised you wanted to visit this porch even on our wedding night."

"This is the place I want to end all of our evenings, watching the sun set and the stars come out... seated in the swing on our porch. Two old married people. Our children tucked safe and sound in their beds upstairs. It's our first tradition. And I hope you aren't disappointed that I wanted our first married night to be in this house? And thanks for understanding and humoring me about staying at your parents' home the past few nights. A silly tradition and all, about grooms not seeing their brides and all, but you went along with it. We're going on that marvelous trip tomorrow, but I just wanted to be here... with you, in *our* house as we begin our married life. You don't mind too much do you?"

His fingers slid slowly along her skin to caress her cheek

as she gazed up at him. "If you had wanted to stay on a horse blanket in the barn out back, I would have agreed. As long as I finally get to have you in my arms all night then it doesn't matter where we are."

"I love you, Cole Drayton. You've given me more than I ever hoped to find in my life, the day I came to this house."

"I love you, Emma Drayton. You brought me back to life the day you dumped me out of my bed in the middle of the night. I knew you were going to be trouble... I just didn't know then how much I would come to *love* that trouble." His words and devilish grin brought much the same from her.

Just as his head was bending towards hers, she abruptly stood, the quilt sliding from her shoulders onto the swing's seat. "Think you can carry me across that threshold once more?"

A shimmering glitter of heat filled the gaze he centered on her as he rose to stand in front of her, accepting her challenge. In a quick movement, he had her in his arms and her feet lifted off the porch. Her arms went around his neck and she laughed with joy.

"I don't *think* I can do it, I know it. And I will carry you up those stairs, too. I haven't been practicing lifting hay bales in the barn for nothing. I figured my southern bride might expect no less than her groom to do his best impression of Rhett Butler on our wedding night and carry you up the staircase."

She leaned in and captured his mouth with hers. What started out to be a teasing kiss was quickly changed in a heartbeat as his lips took control and drew her into a heat of a fire that built into a blaze within her in seconds. The fireworks of the evening were supplied in his kiss.

Emma drew back only enough to meet his fevered gaze. A slow smile curved her mouth.

"Talk is overrated. So, show me what you got, cowboy."

Cole didn't miss a step as he carried her into the house, pausing to shut the door with his boot heel, and then up the steps he went and, at the top, he paused only long enough to claim another kiss. And then he proceeded to show her just what a cowboy who held the world in his arms could do!

THE END

The Texas Lawmen Series

The three sexiest lawmen ever to wear a badge. Two of them wear the silver star of the elite Texas Rangers. One is a United States Federal Marshal. Besides having the law in common, they are good friends with their friendships having been forged over the years. They keep their bonds of friendship and have each other's backs whenever needed. Dedicated to duty and their badges, their private lives are solitary ones until the day each of them meets their match in the opposite sex.

Book 1: *Beware the Ranger*

Book 2: *The Lawman's Apache Moon*

Book 3: *Along Came a Ranger*

Book 4: The Sheriff's Christmas Angels

Available now at your favorite online retailer!

ABOUT THE AUTHOR

Born and raised in the Lone Star state of Texas, Debra grew up among horses, cowboys, wide open spaces, and real Texas Rangers. Pride in her state and ancestry knows no bounds and it is these heroes and heroines she loves to write about the most. She also draws upon a variety of life experiences including working with abused children, caring for baby animals at a major zoo, and planning high-end weddings (ah, romance!).

Debra's real pride and joys, however, are her son, an aspiring film actor, and a daughter with aspirations to join the Federal Bureau of Investigation. (more story ideas!) When she isn't busy writing about tall Texans and feisty heroines, she can be found cheering on her Texas Tech Red Raiders, or heading off on another cruise adventure. She read her first romance...Janet Dailey's Fiesta San Antonio, over thirty years ago and became hooked on the genre. Writing contemporary western romances, is both her passion and dream come true, and she hopes her books will bring smiles...and sighs...to all who believe in happily-ever-after's.

Visit her website at www.debraholtbooks.com.

Thank you for reading

THE SHERIFF'S CHRISTMAS ANGELS

If you enjoyed this book, you can find more from all our great authors at TulePublishing.com, or from your favorite online retailer.

Printed in the USA
CPSIA information can be obtained
at www.ICGtesting.com
LVHW050804170324
774682LV00040B/1065